Pizza-Man Be Yourself.

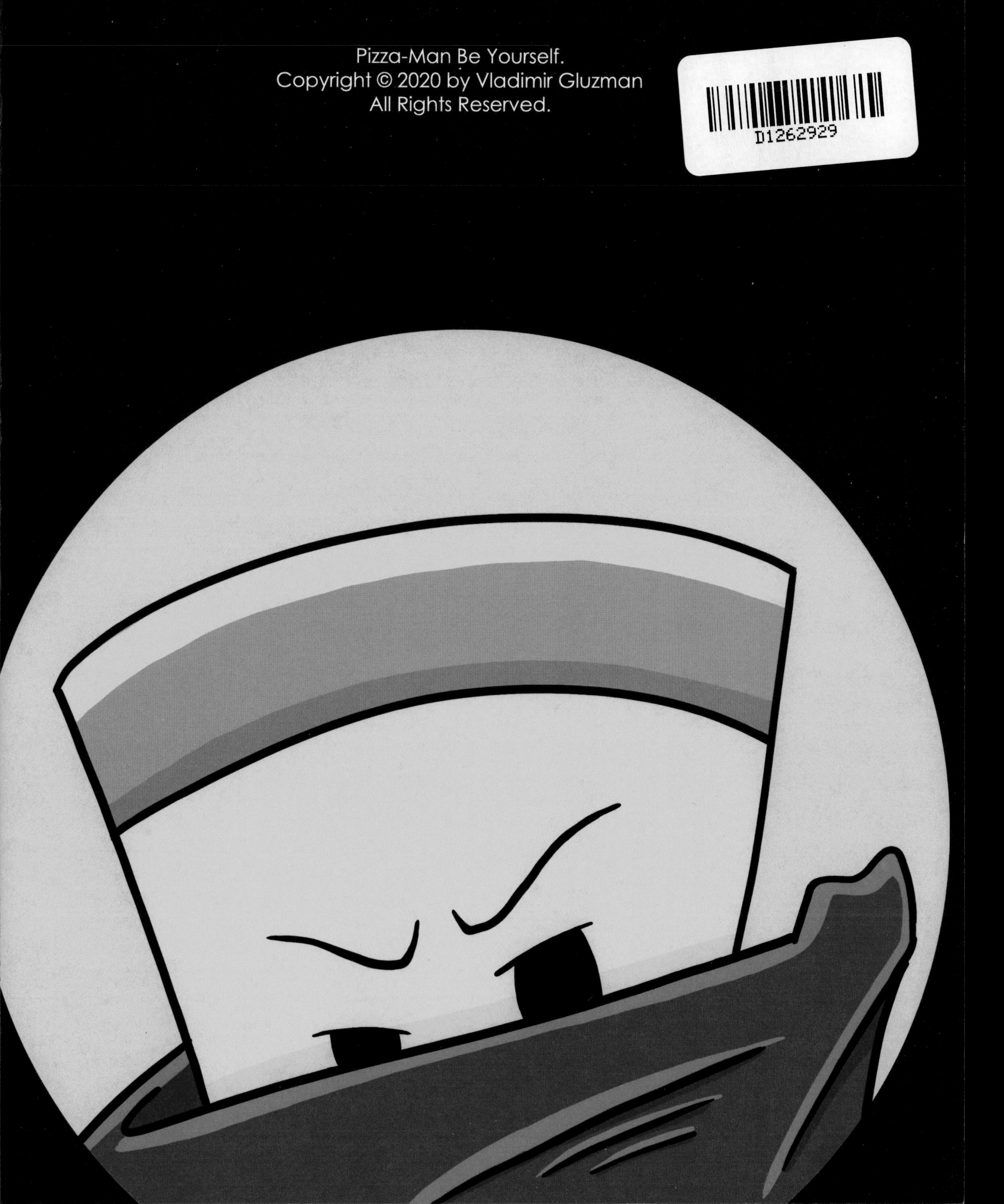

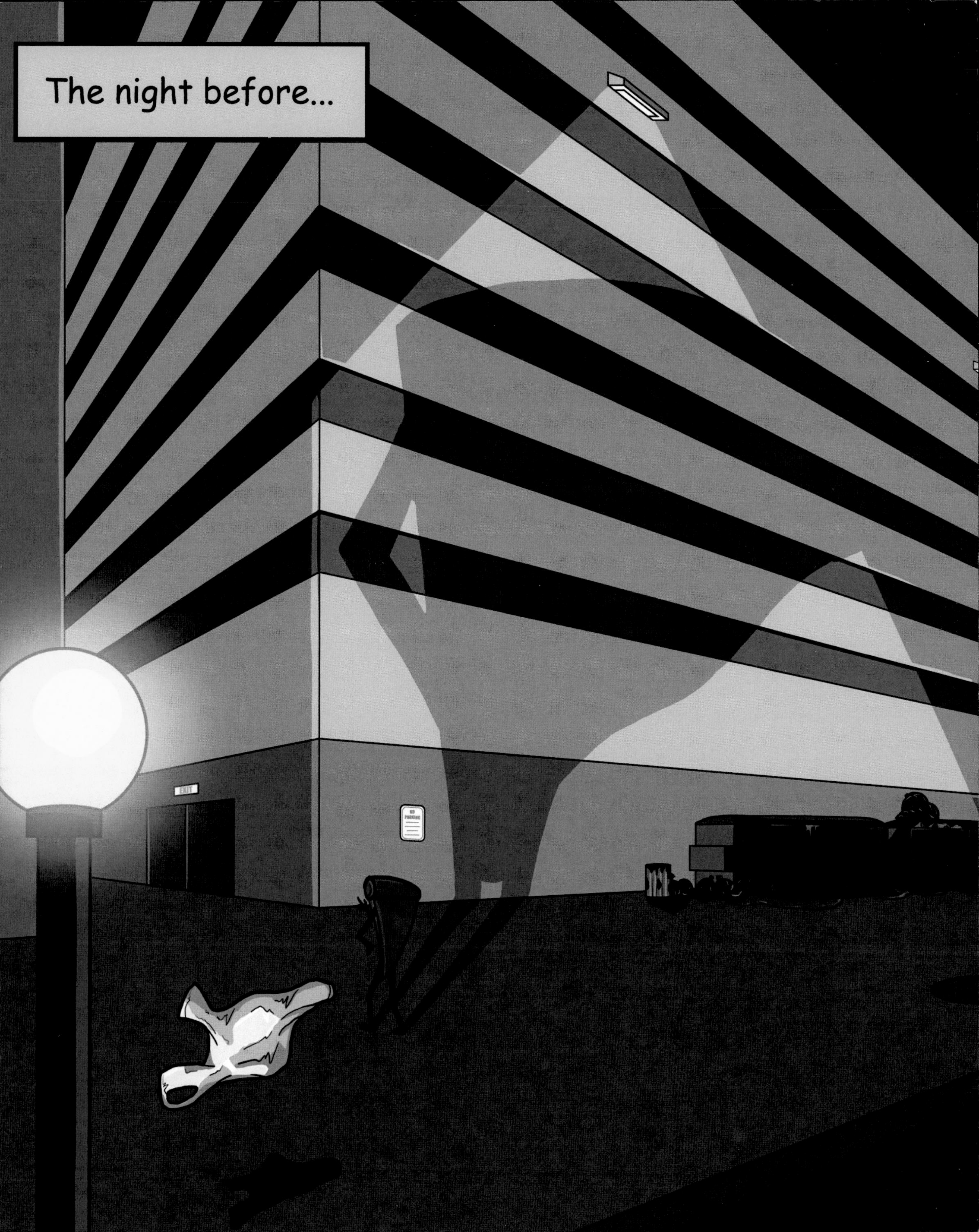
The night before...
EXIT

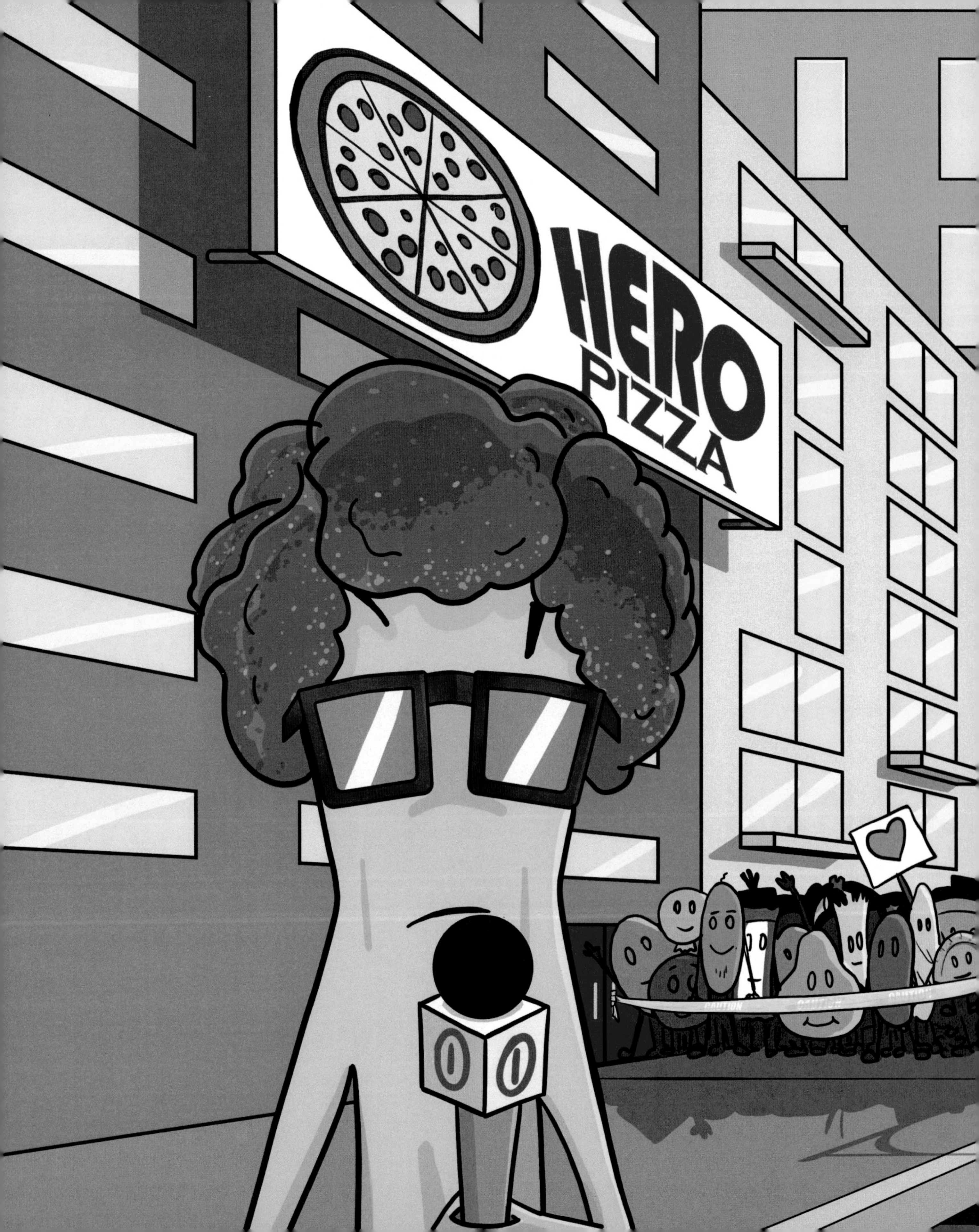
HERO
PIZZA

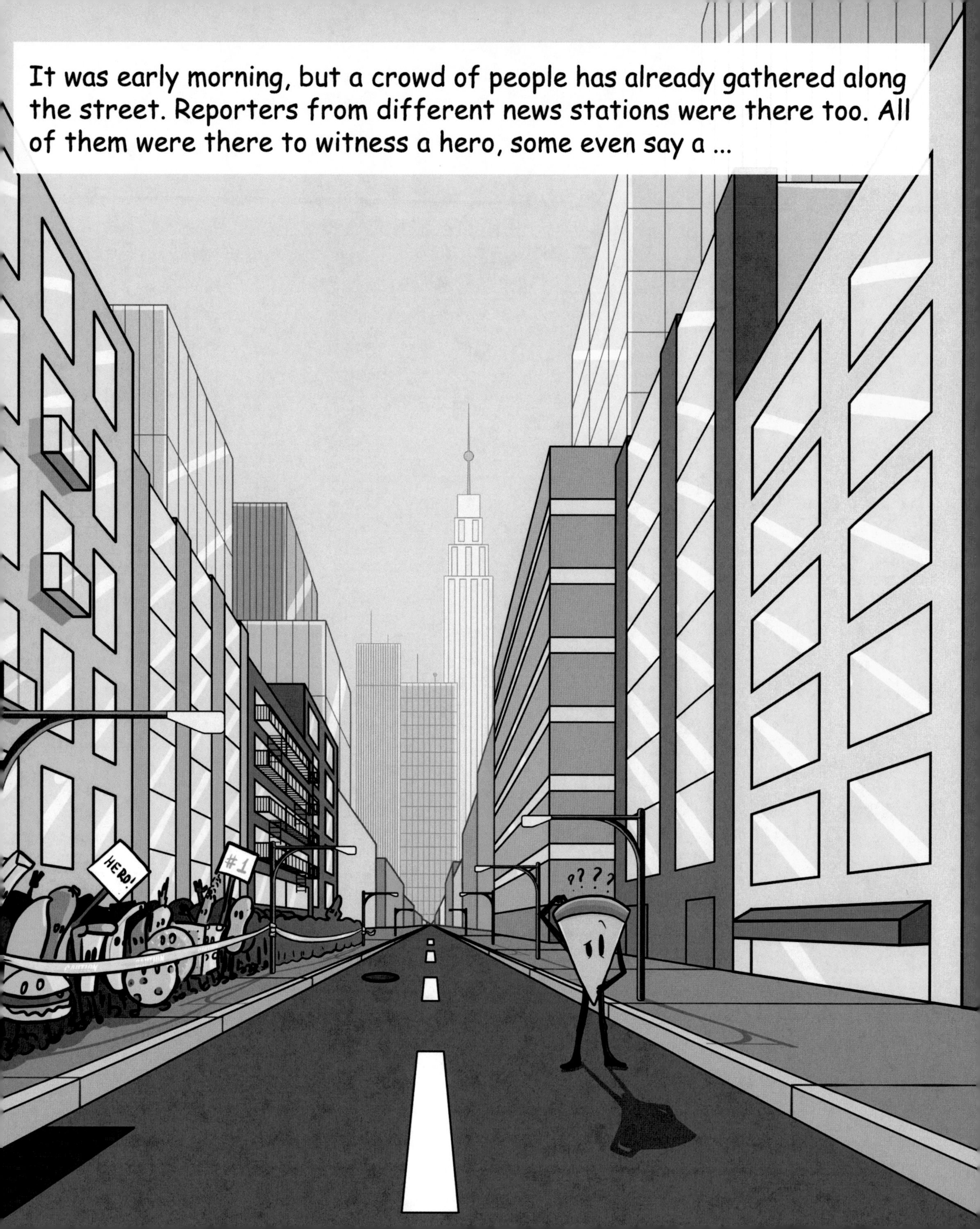
It was early morning, but a crowd of people has already gathered along the street. Reporters from different news stations were there too. All of them were there to witness a hero, some even say a ...
HERO!
#1
????

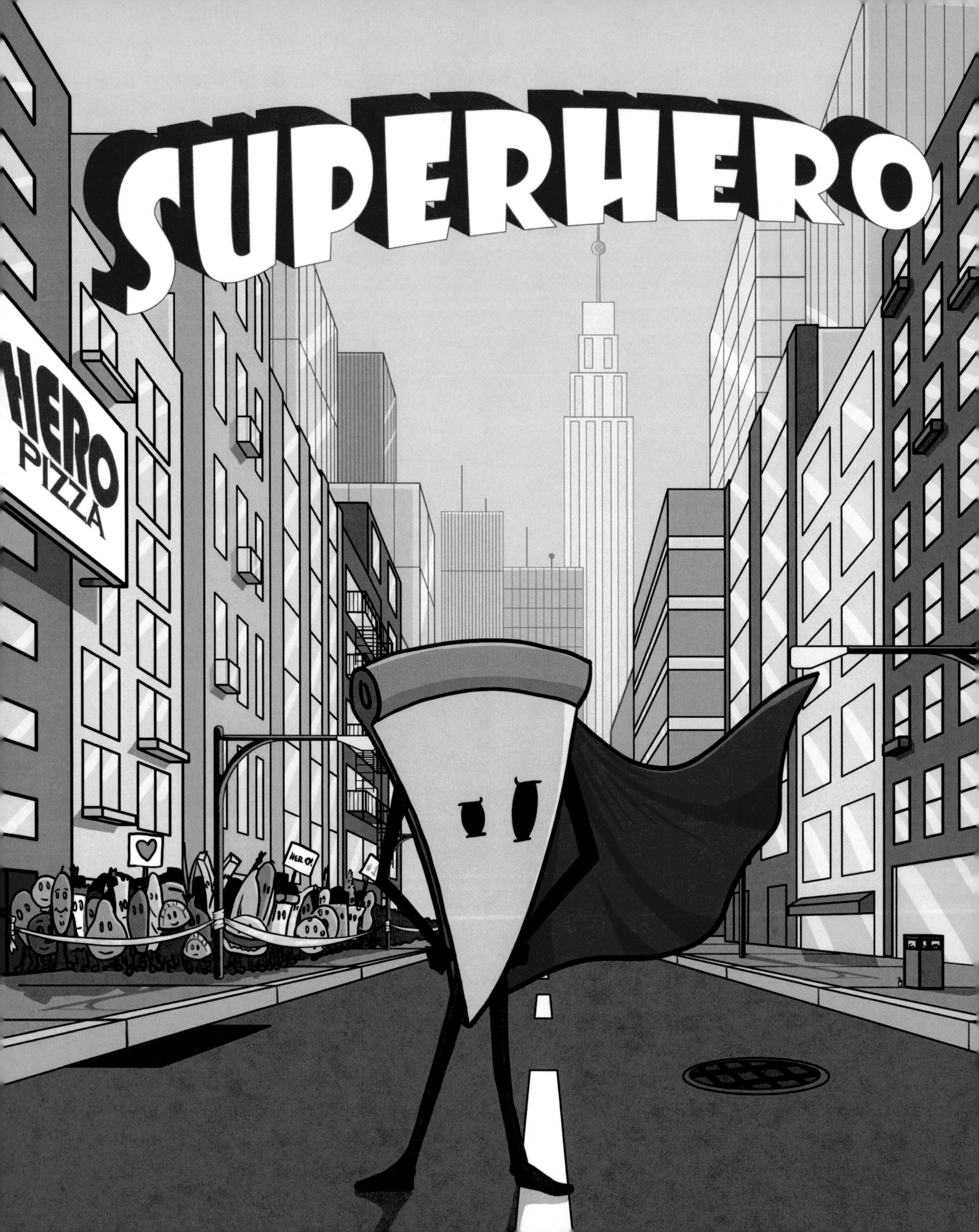
SUPERHERO
HERO
PIZZA
HER O!
#1

The hero stood in the middle of a street, he looked puzzled and out of place. The reporters with their cameras and microphones surrounded the hero, all asking questions.
"Who are you? Where are you from? What are your powers?"

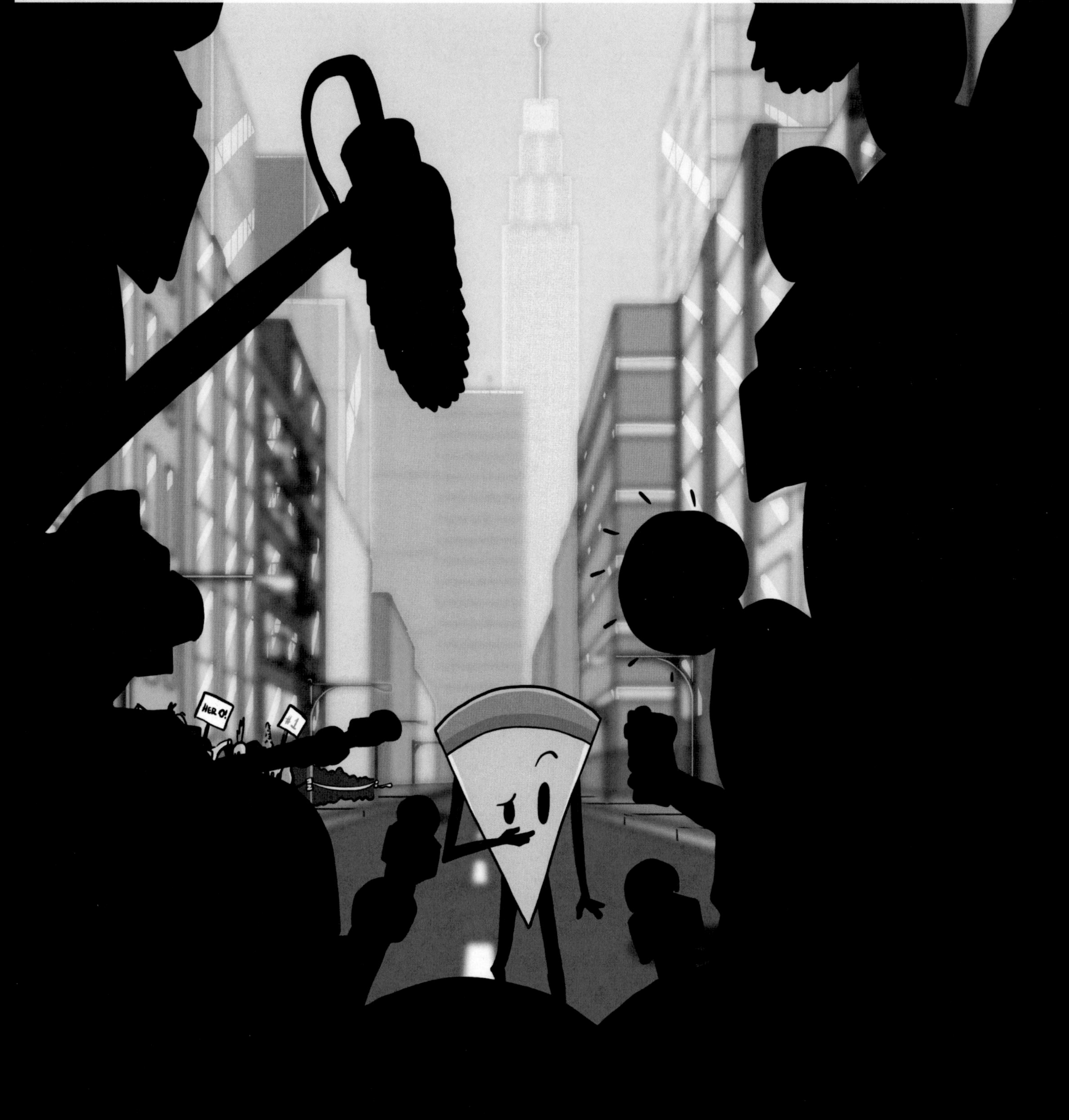

Truth is he was not a superhero and didn't have any super powers. He was new to the city and all he wanted was to fit in and maybe make a friend or two.

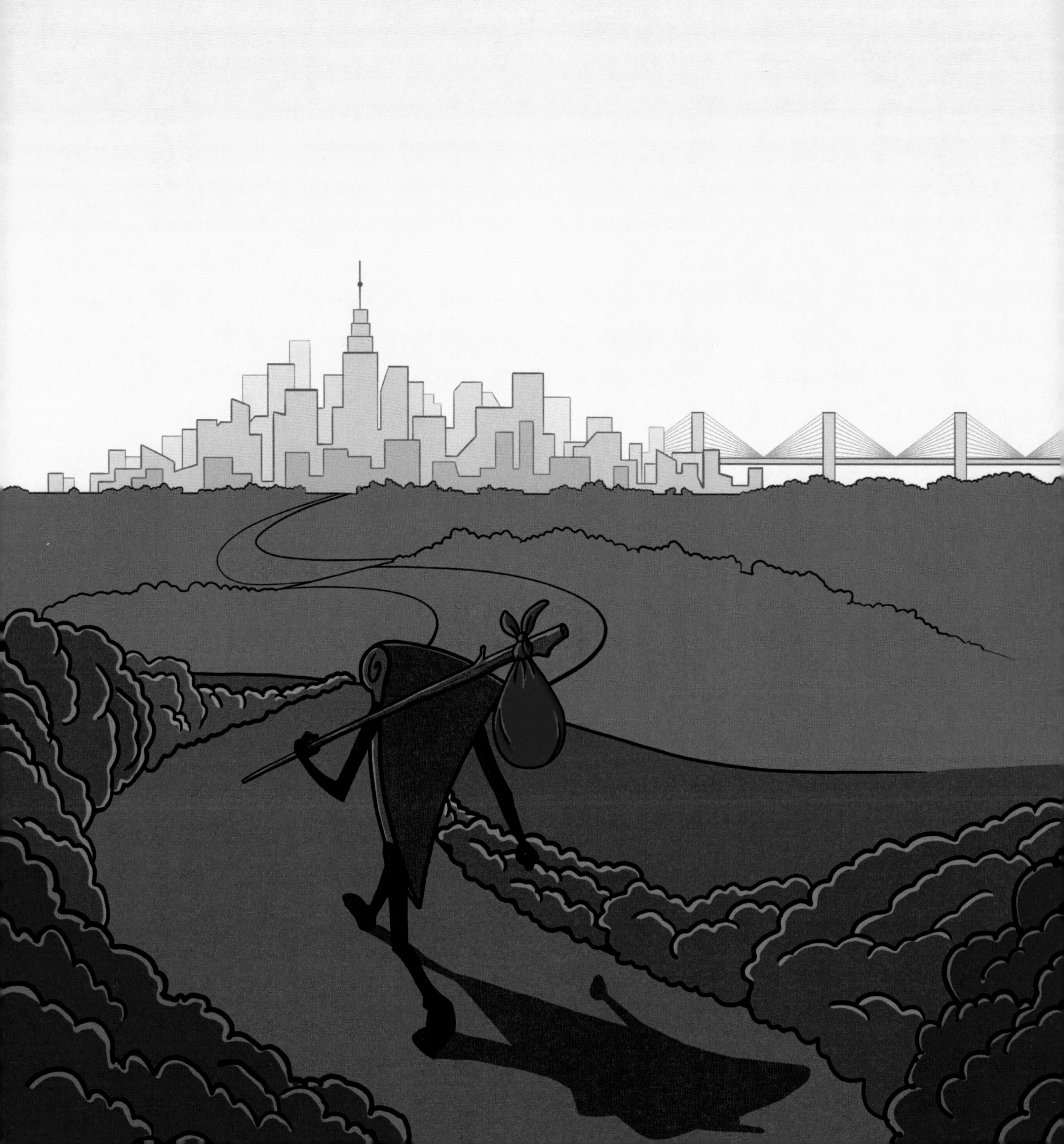

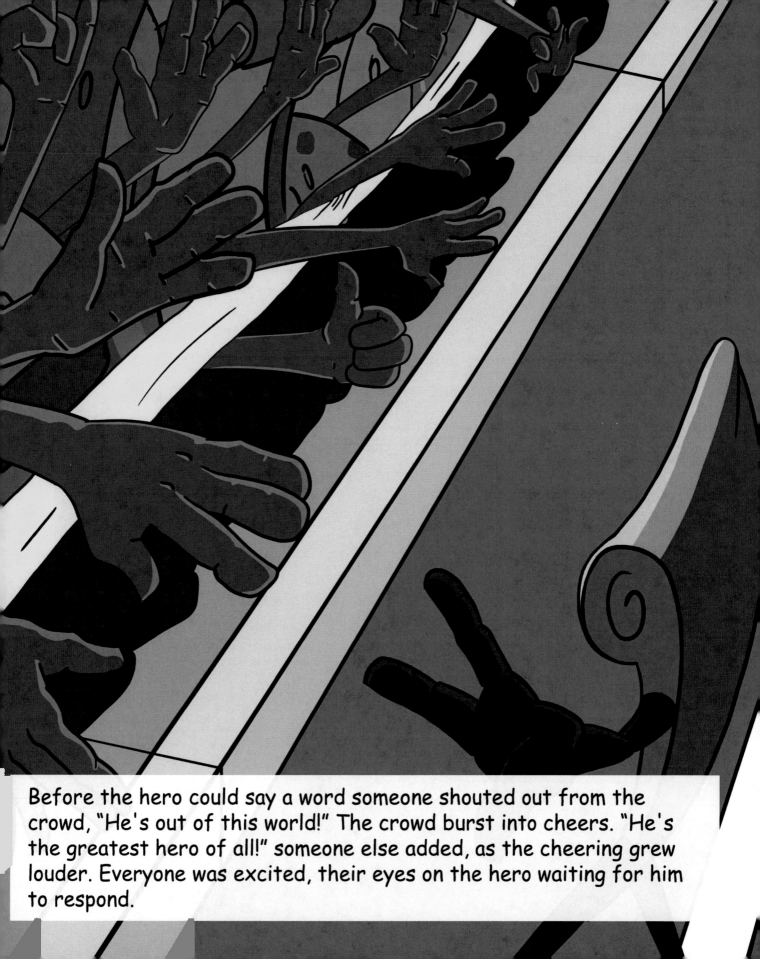

Before the hero could say a word someone shouted out from the crowd, "He's out of this world!" The crowd burst into cheers. "He's the greatest hero of all!" someone else added, as the cheering grew louder. Everyone was excited, their eyes on the hero waiting for him to respond.

Everyone was talking at the same time and cheering was getting louder and louder. It got so loud that the hero could no longer make out what was said. Everyone's expectations of him began to overwhelm him and he felt a little bit uneasy. Unsure what to do next he did the worst thing he could've done, he decided to make up a story.

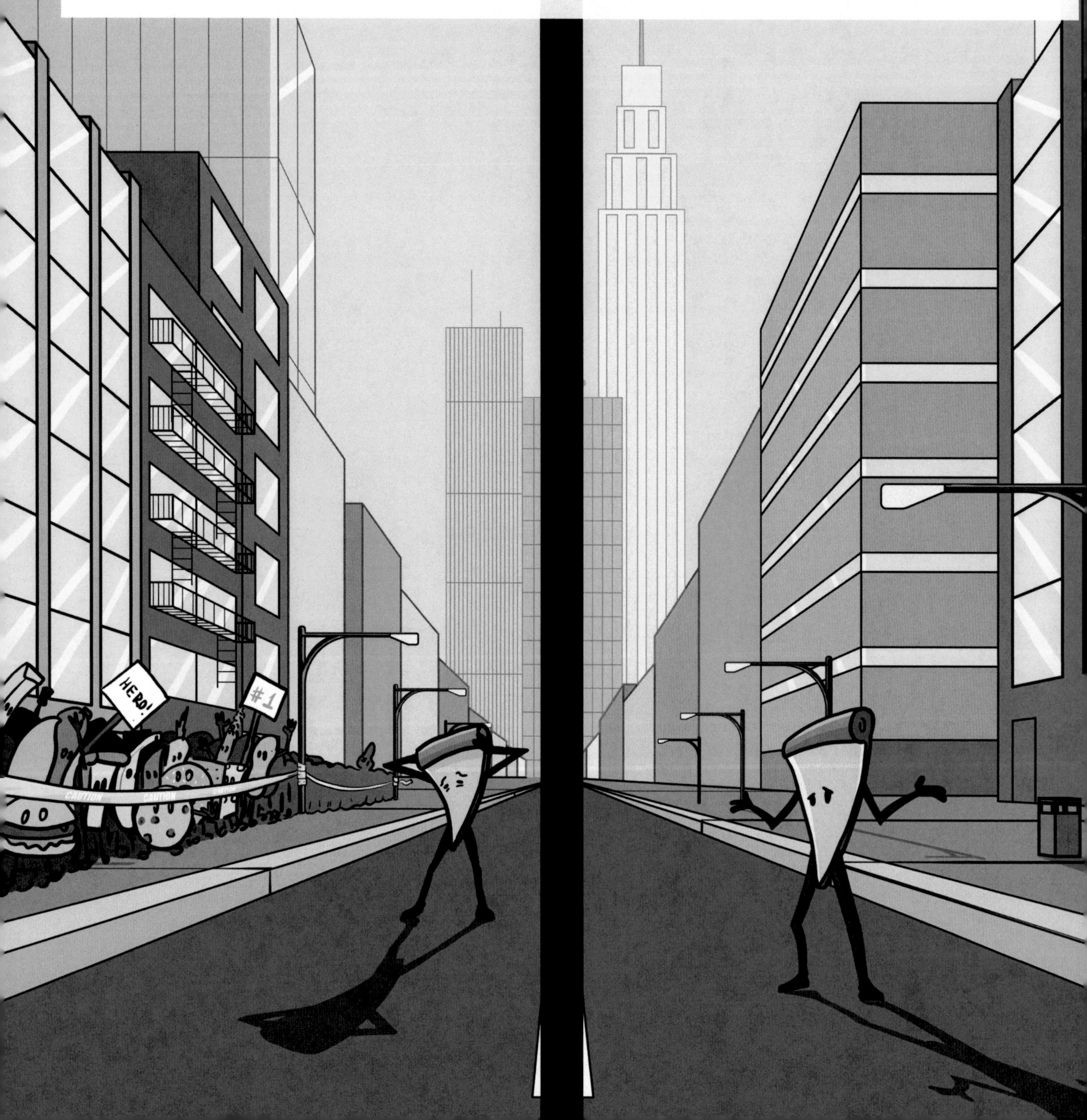
HERO!
#1

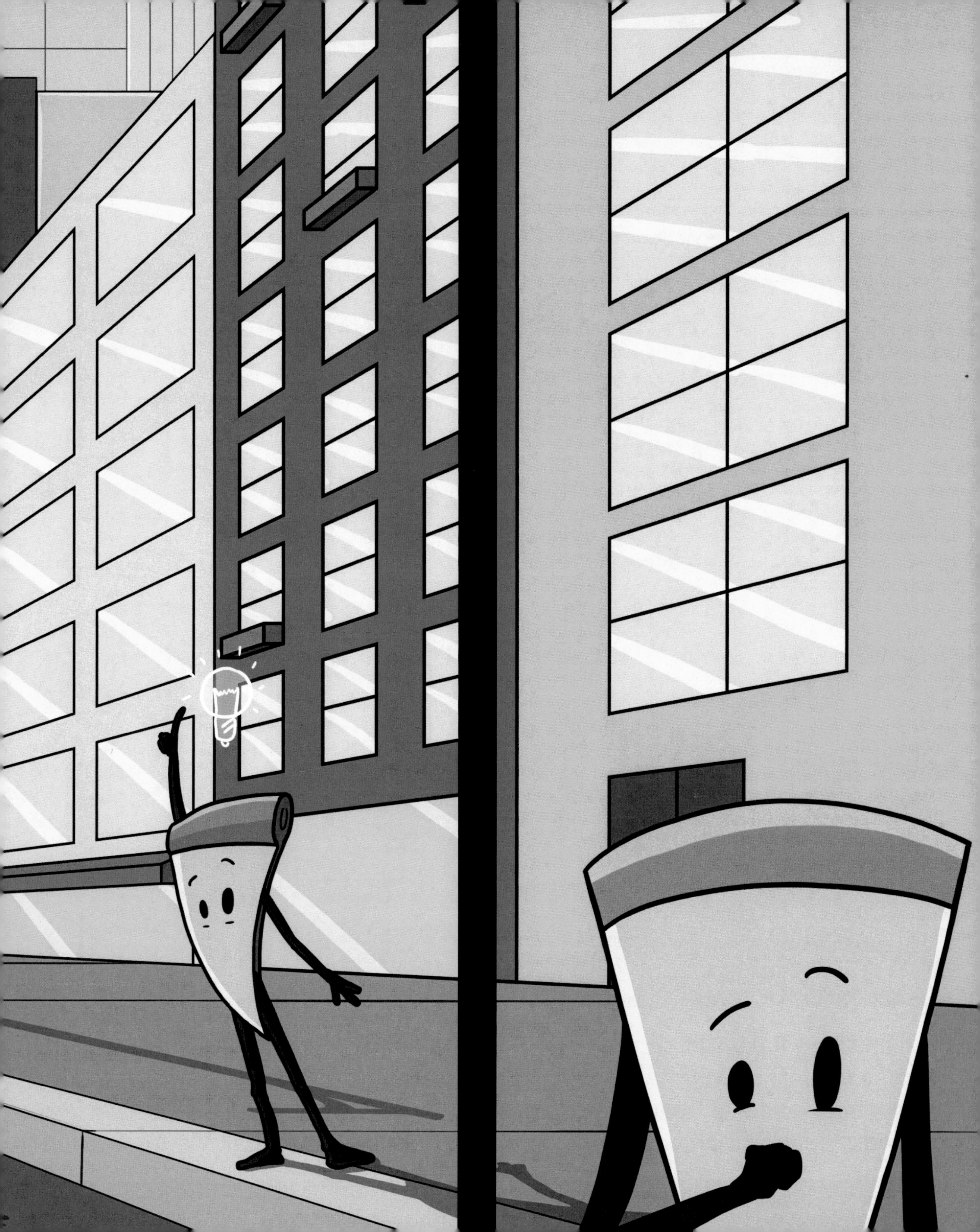

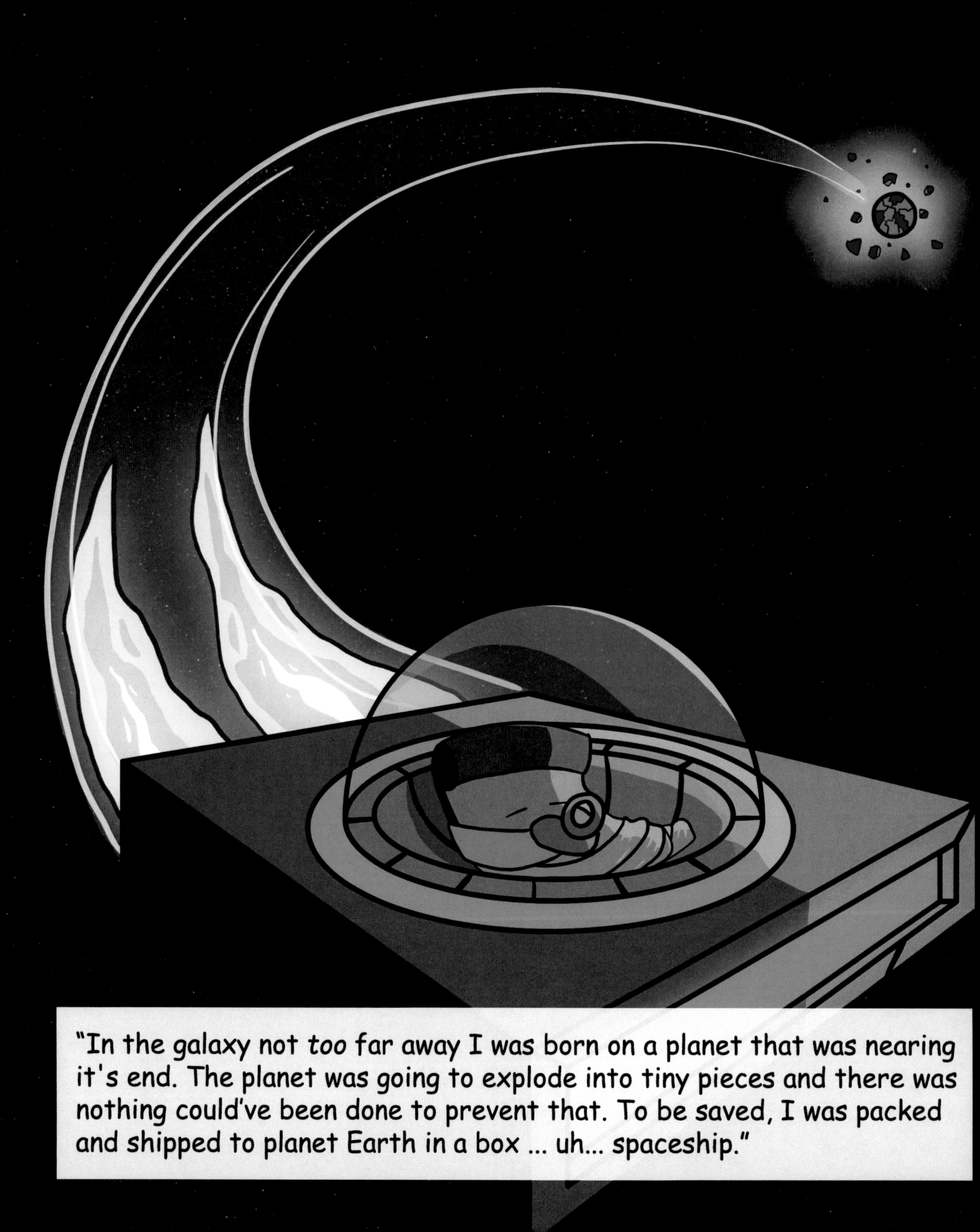
"In the galaxy not *too* far away I was born on a planet that was nearing it's end. The planet was going to explode into tiny pieces and there was nothing could've been done to prevent that. To be saved, I was packed and shipped to planet Earth in a box ... uh... spaceship."

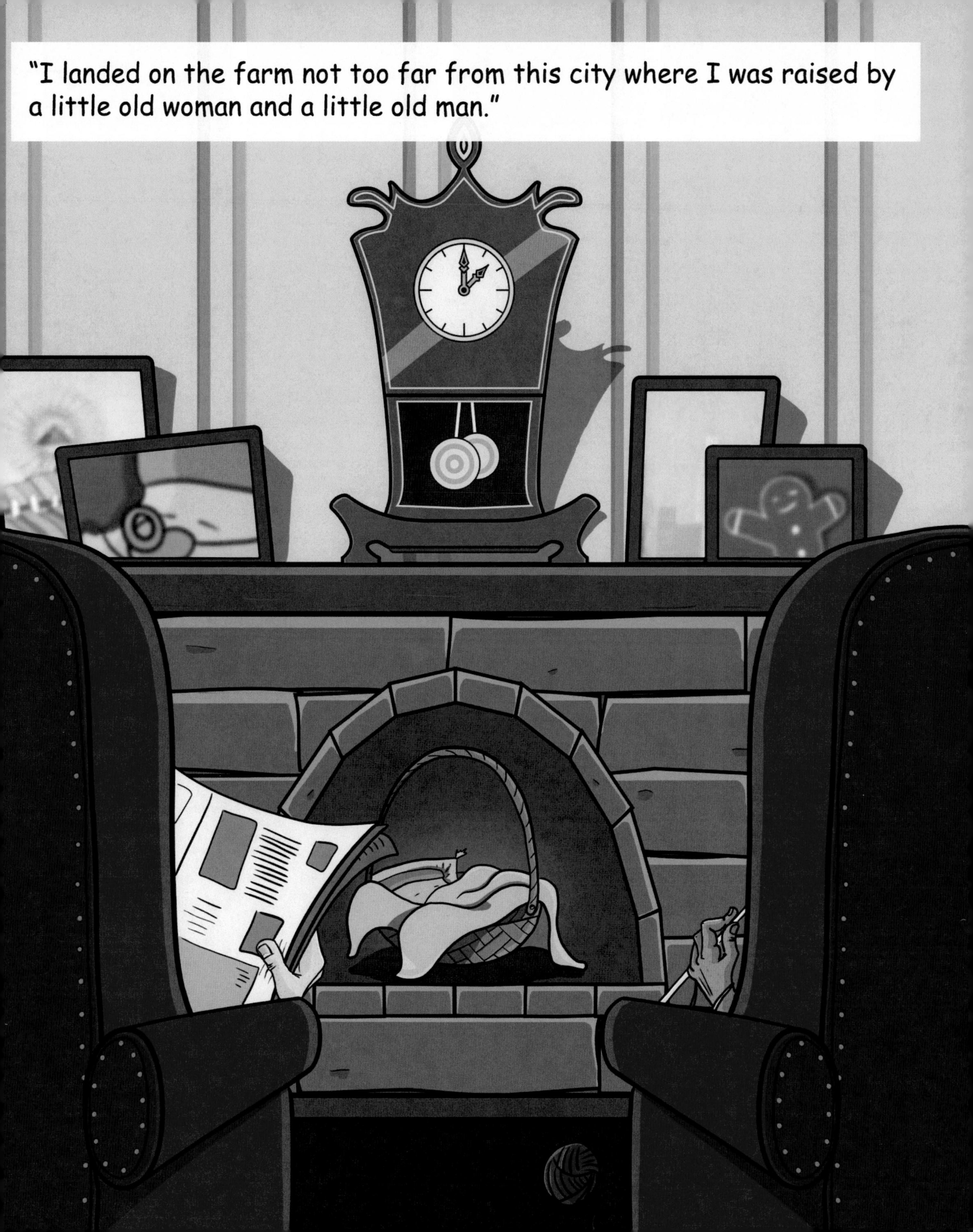
"I landed on the farm not too far from this city where I was raised by a little old woman and a little old man."

"Now, this all sounds great, but it needs a little bit of action," the hero thought to himself.

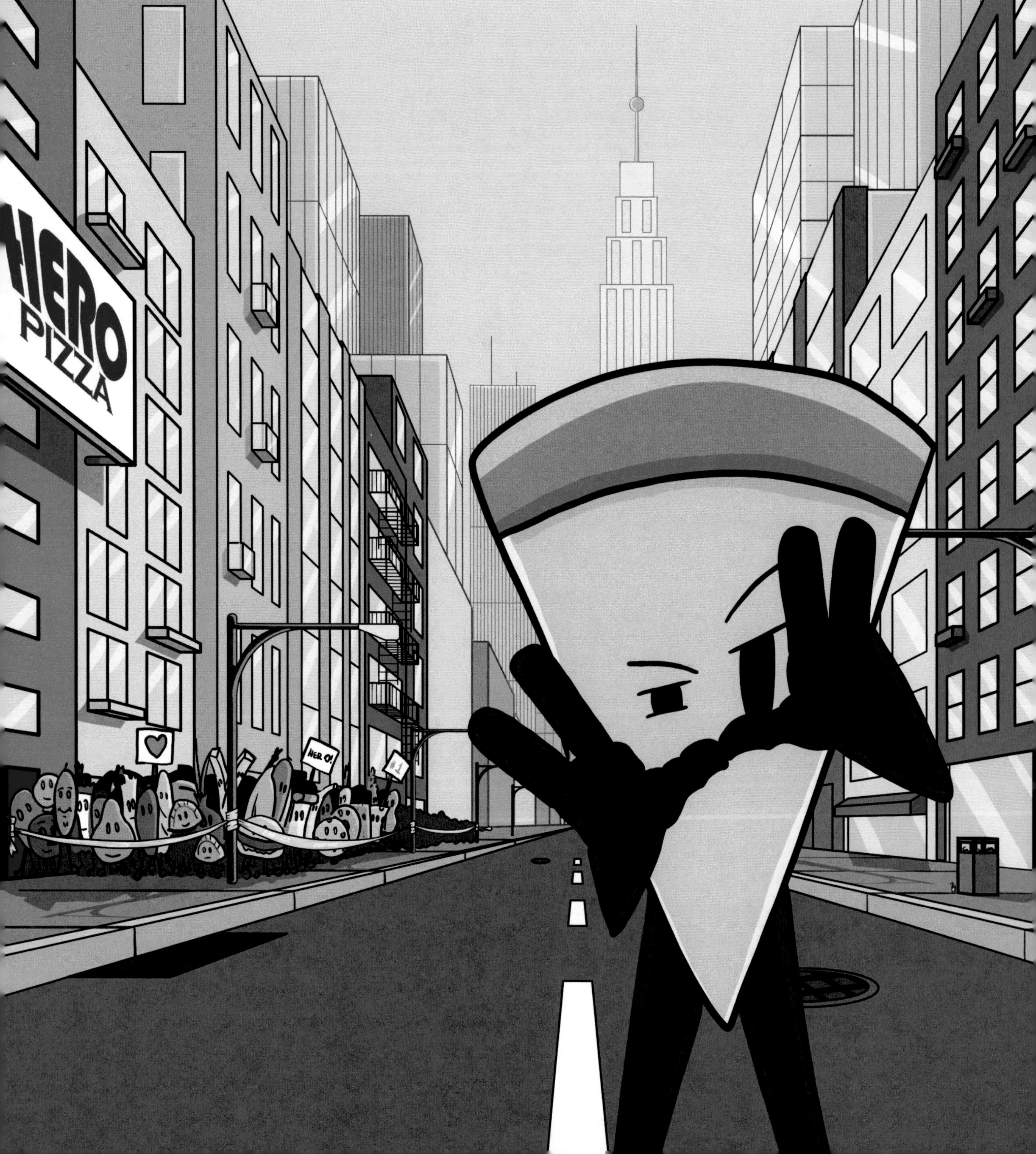
HERO
PIZZA

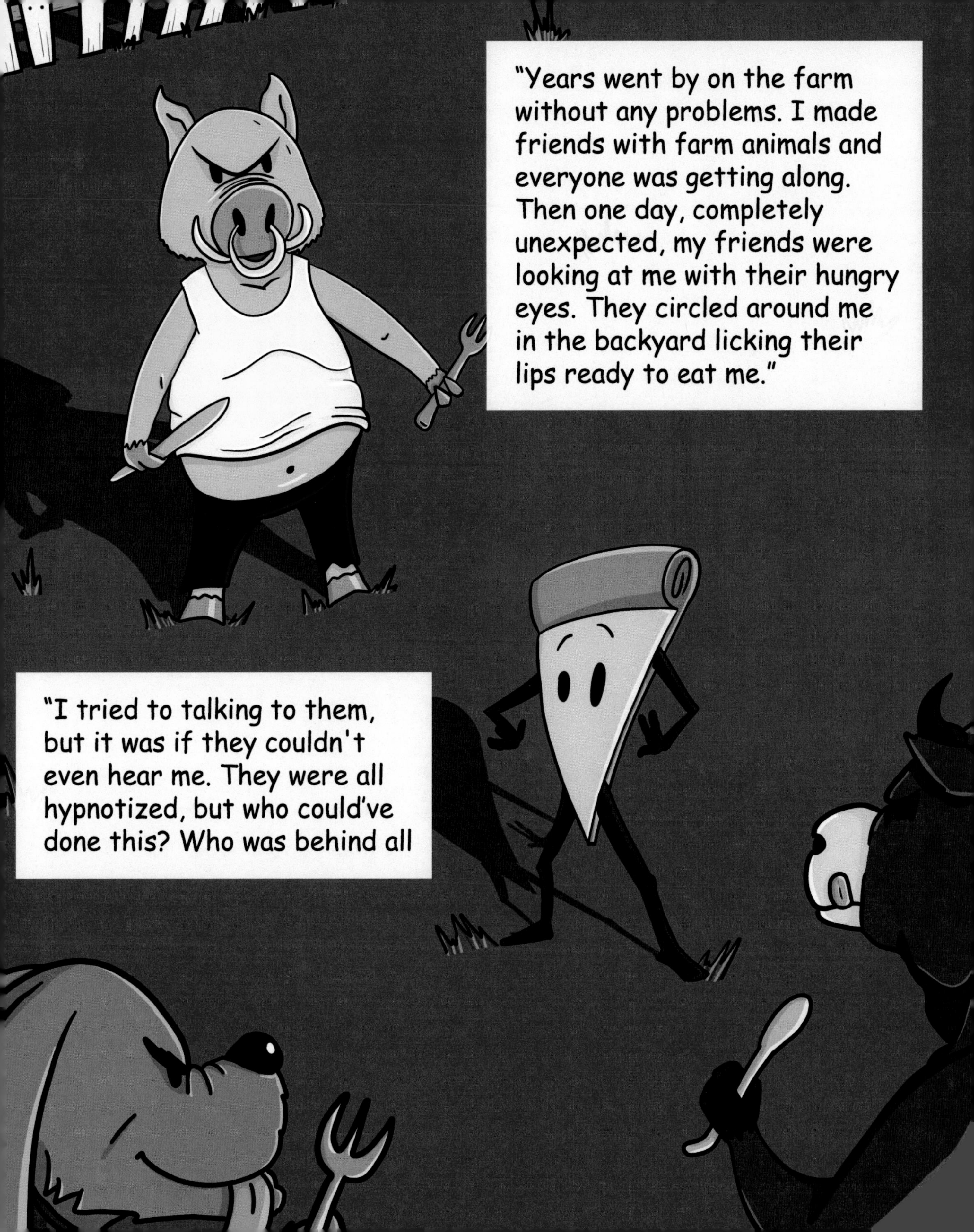
"Years went by on the farm without any problems. I made friends with farm animals and everyone was getting along. Then one day, completely unexpected, my friends were looking at me with their hungry eyes. They circled around me in the backyard licking their lips ready to eat me."
"I tried to talking to them, but it was if they couldn't even hear me. They were all hypnotized, but who could've done this? Who was behind all

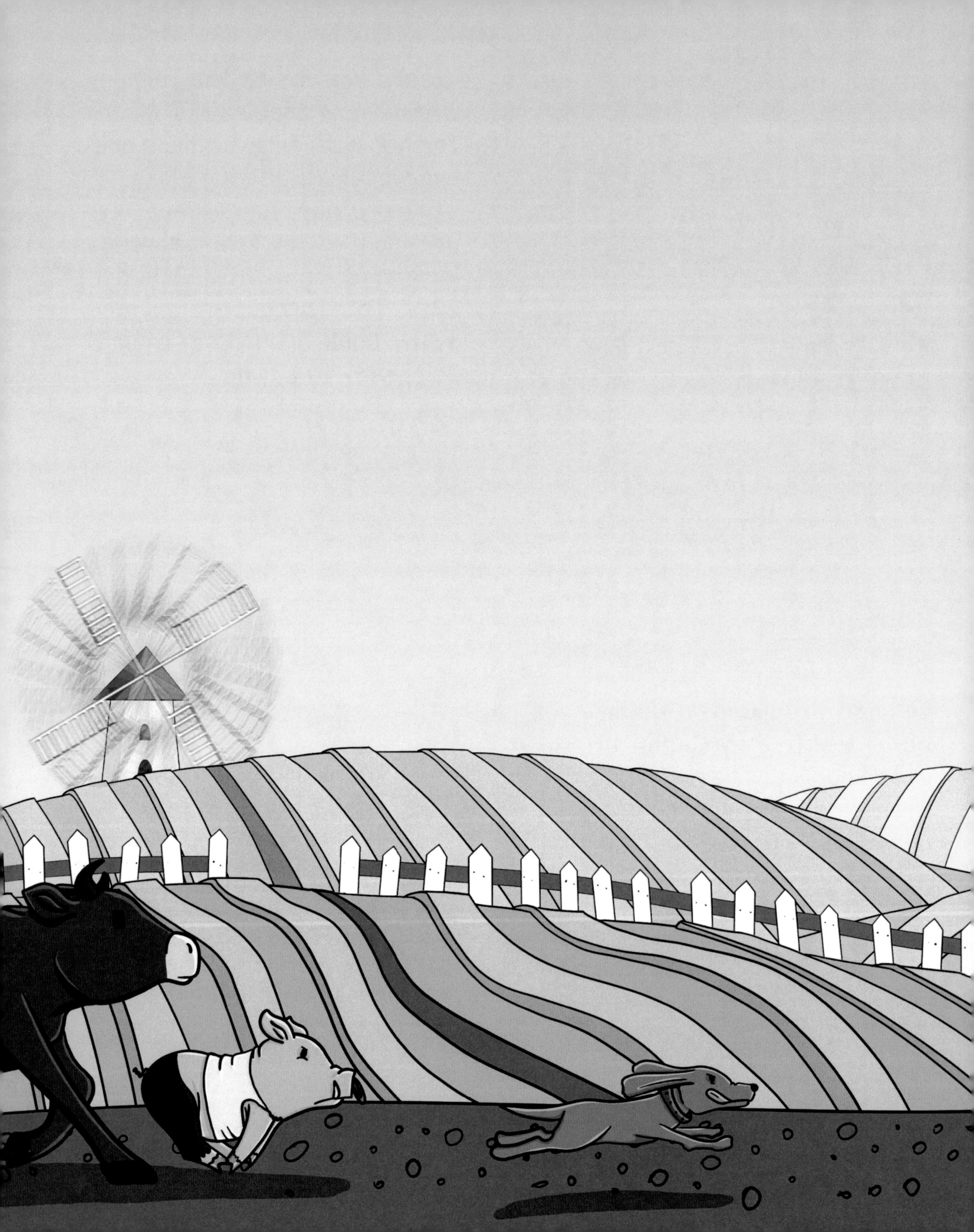

“I had to find whoever was responsible and I was not going to hurt my friends, so running away was my only choice. I ran and ran as fast as I could, I ran past the cow and the pig and the dog and the ... horse?”

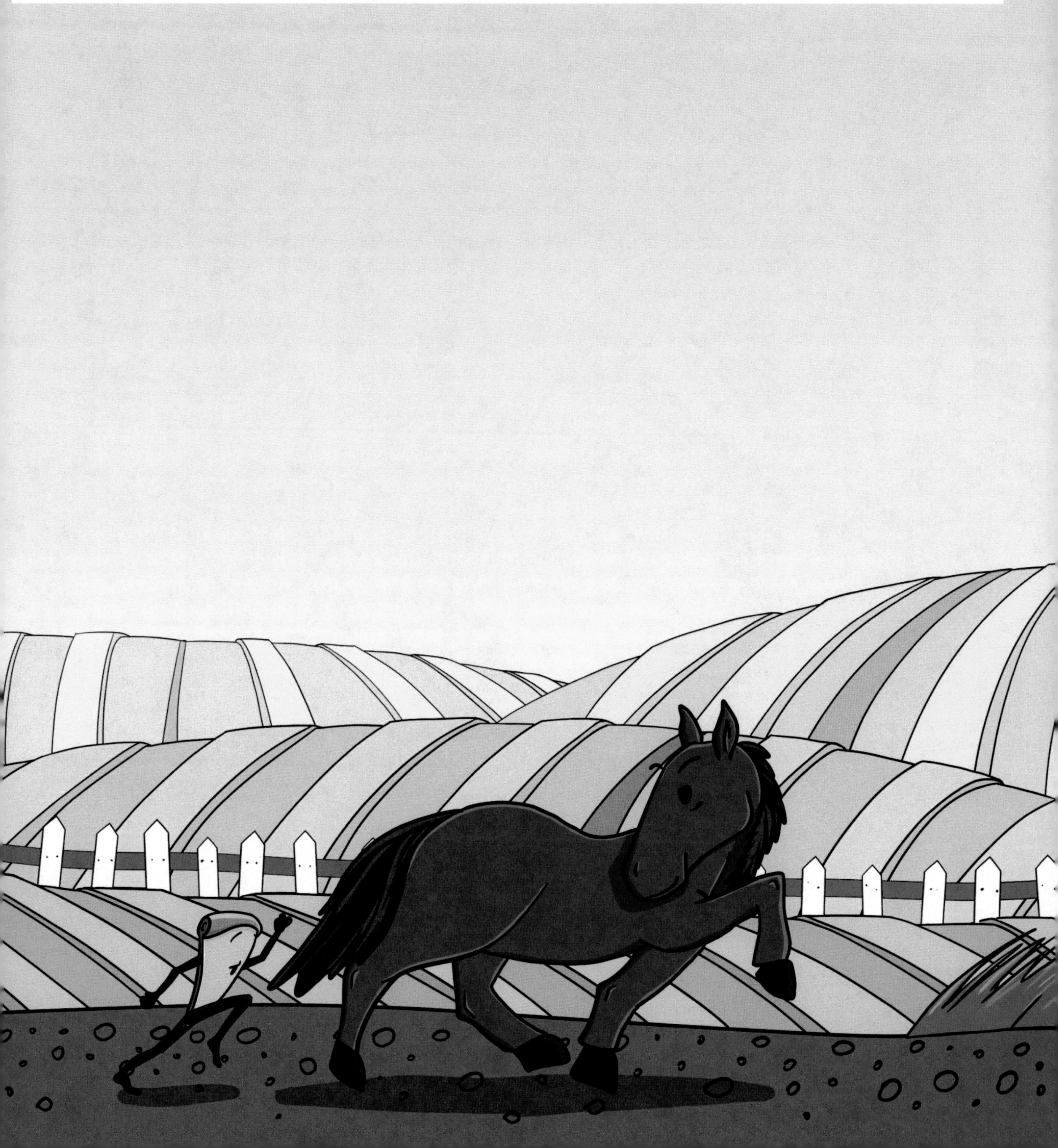

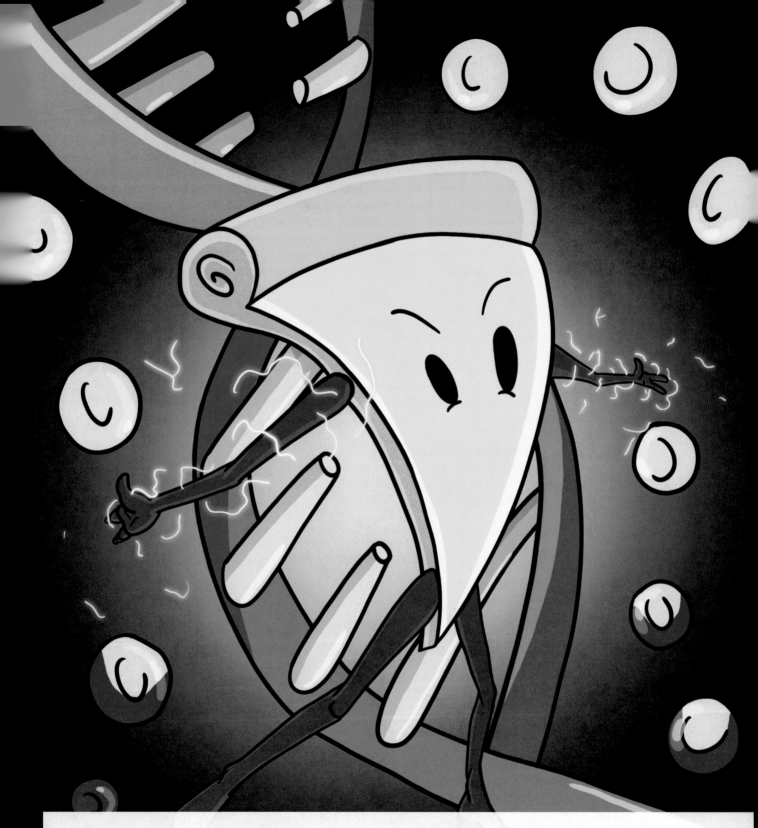

"Very unlikely" he paused.
"Unless! If a superhero everyone wants, then a superhero everyone gets. A superhero with a power of speed faster than light!"

"With my new super power I ran past the cow, the pig, the dog and even the horse was left in a dust."

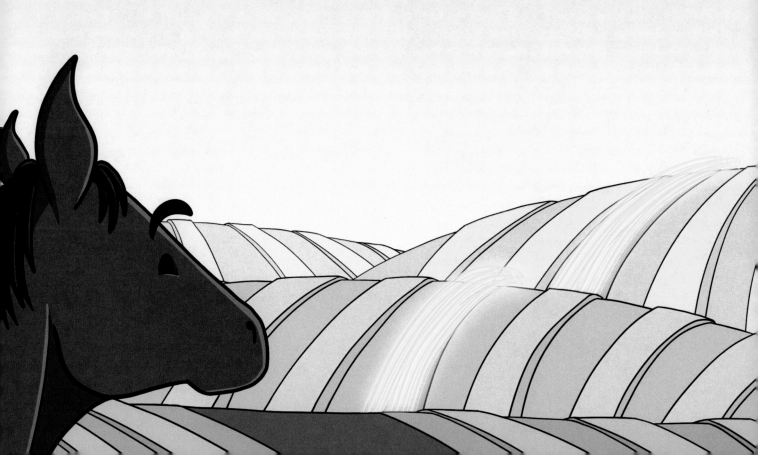

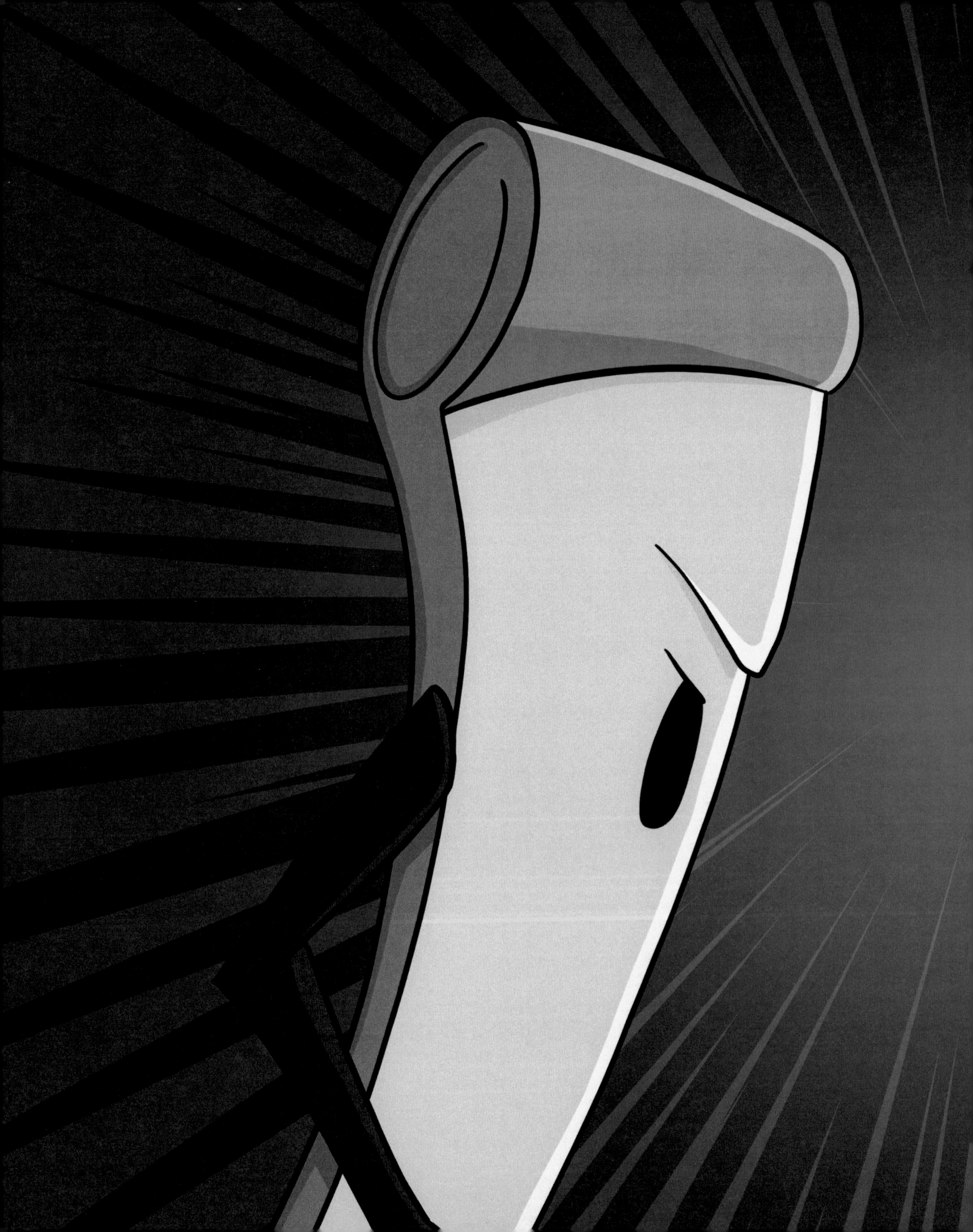

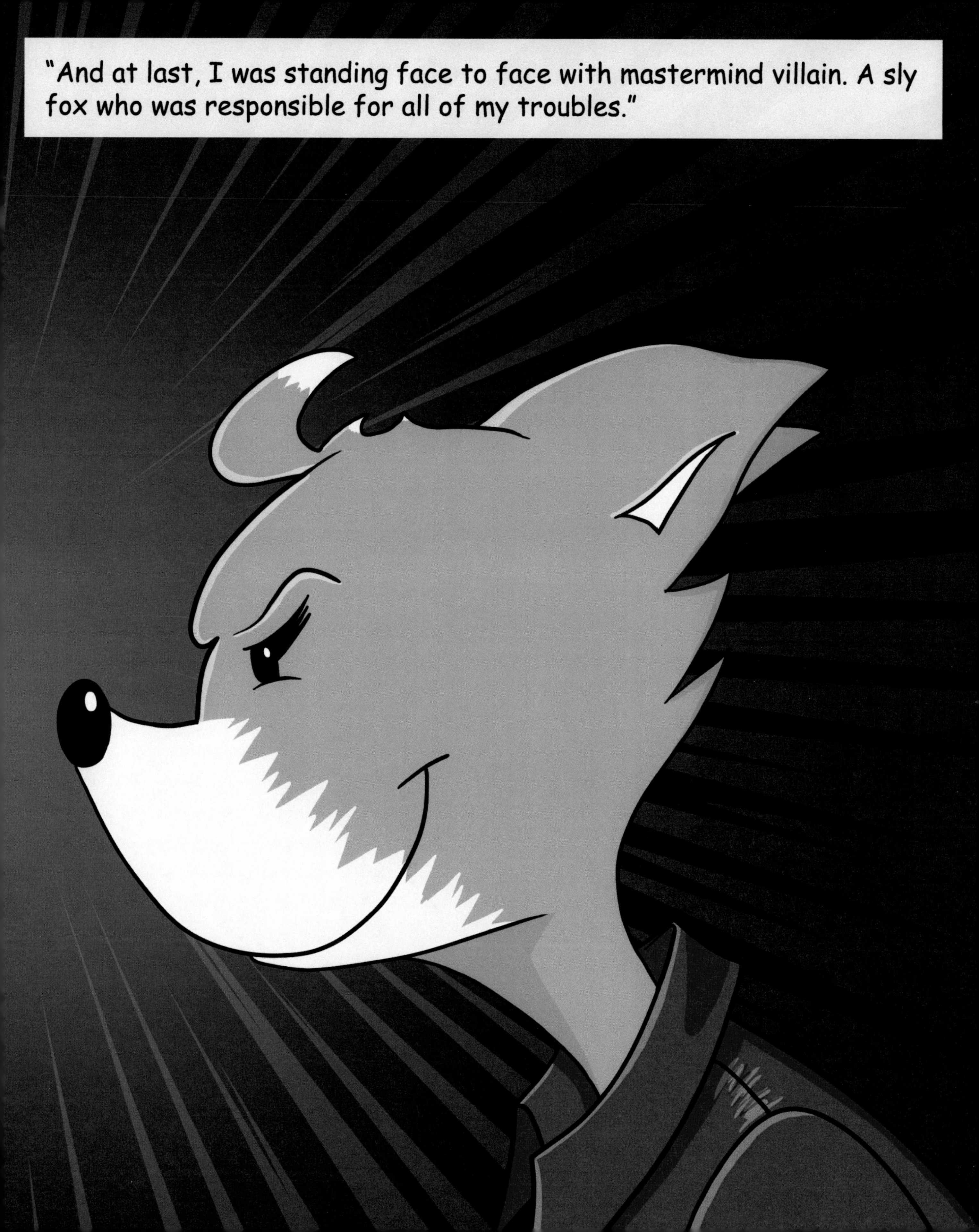
"And at last, I was standing face to face with mastermind villain. A sly fox who was responsible for all of my troubles."

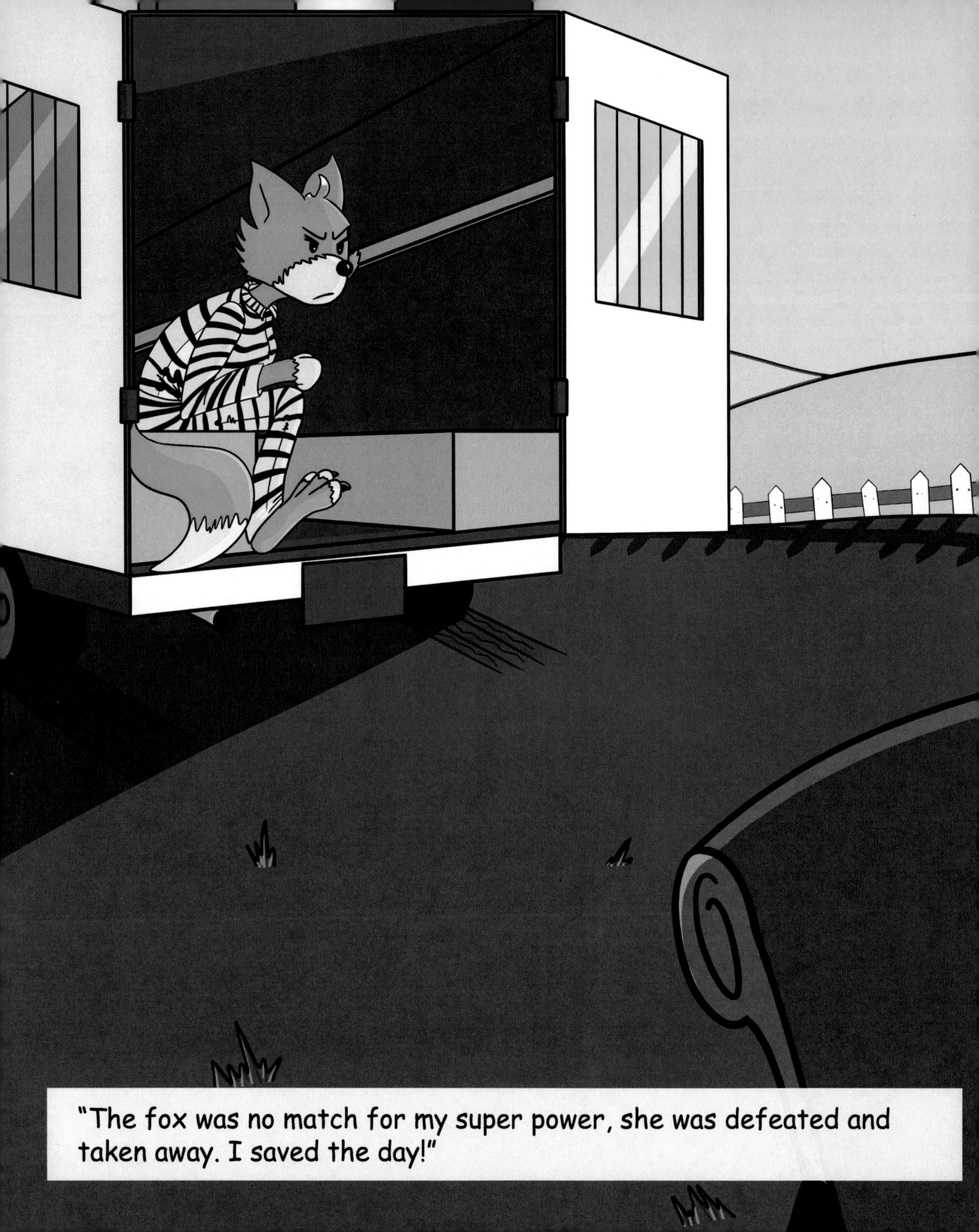

"The fox was no match for my super power, she was defeated and taken away. I saved the day!"

"That all sounds great, but is it really enough? Would defeating a fox make me look like a hero in everyone's eyes? No. No. No. It can't be a fox. It has to be meaner. It has to be stronger. I know, it was a big ... "

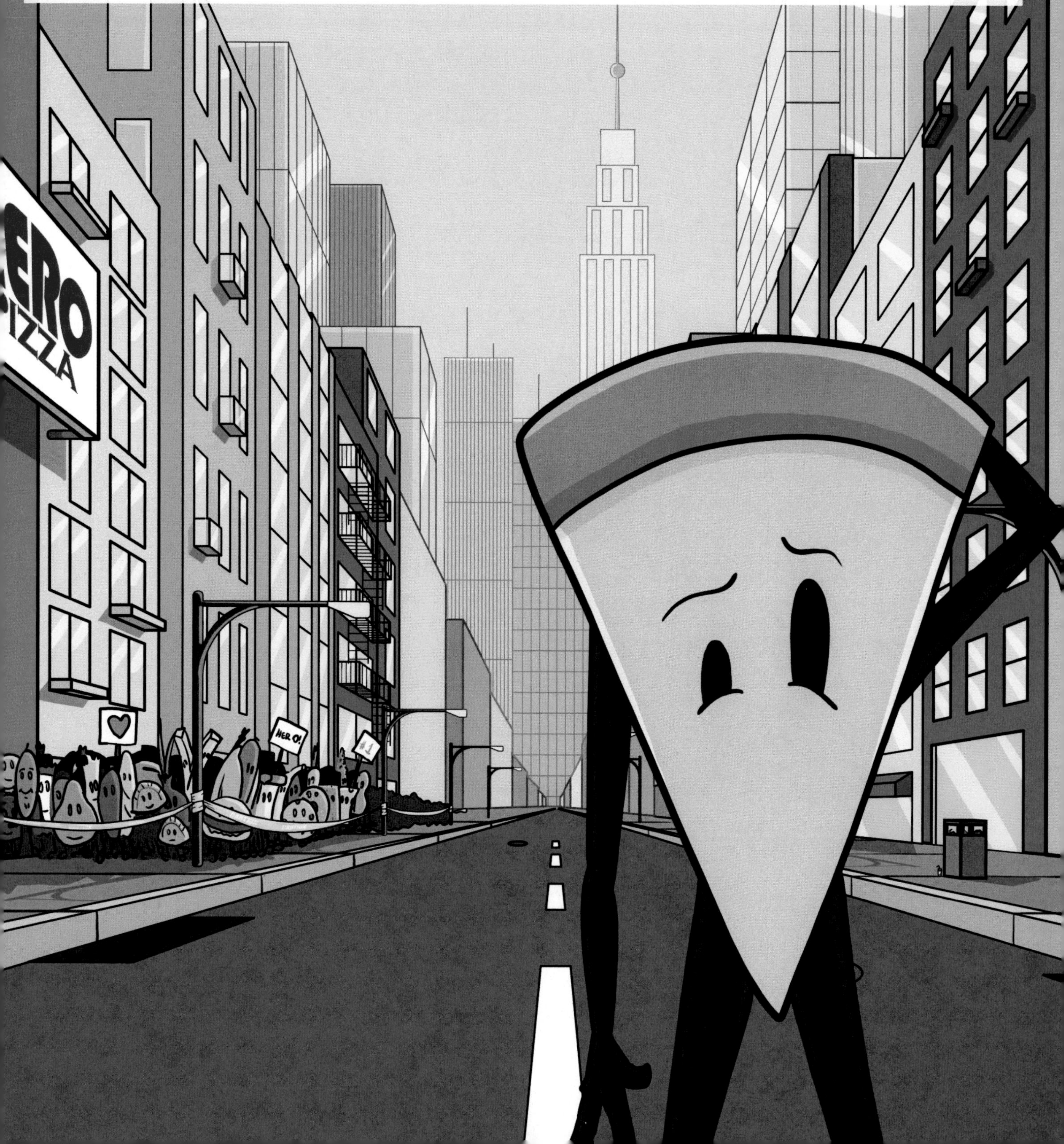
ERO
IZZA
HER O!
#1

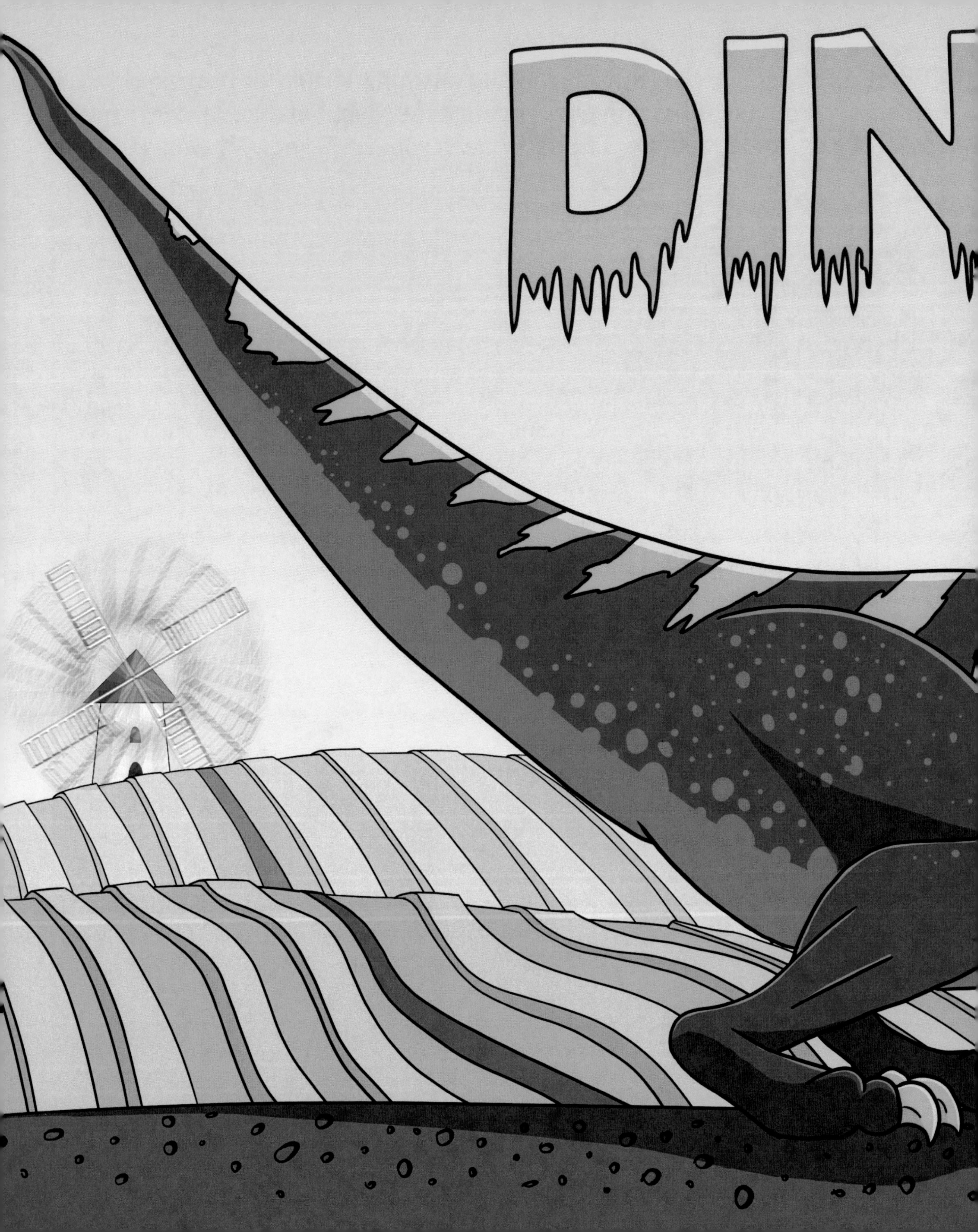
DIN

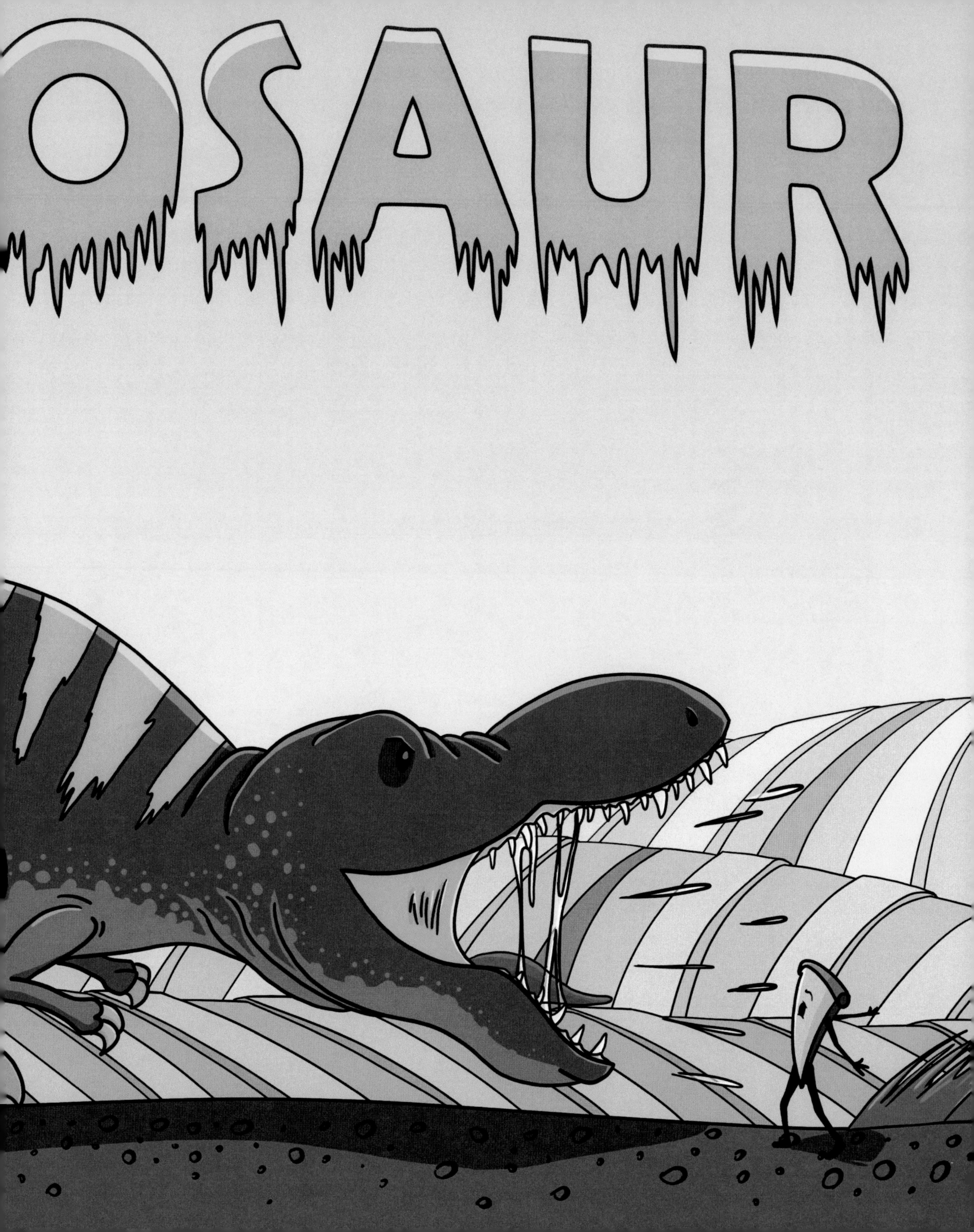
OSAUR

"Now that is a great villain! Except for one problem, with jaws so big and so strong he could swallow me whole without even chewing."

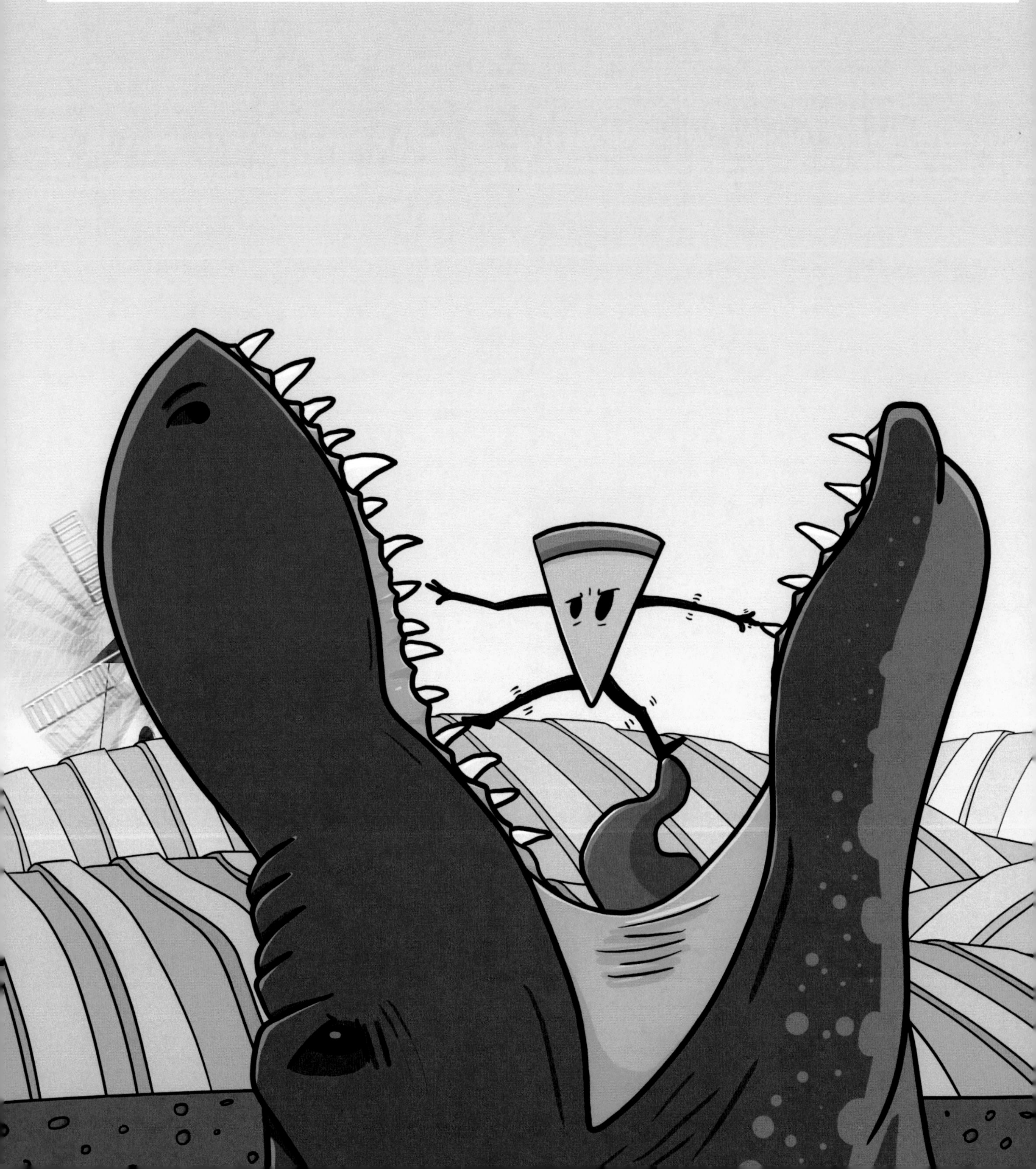

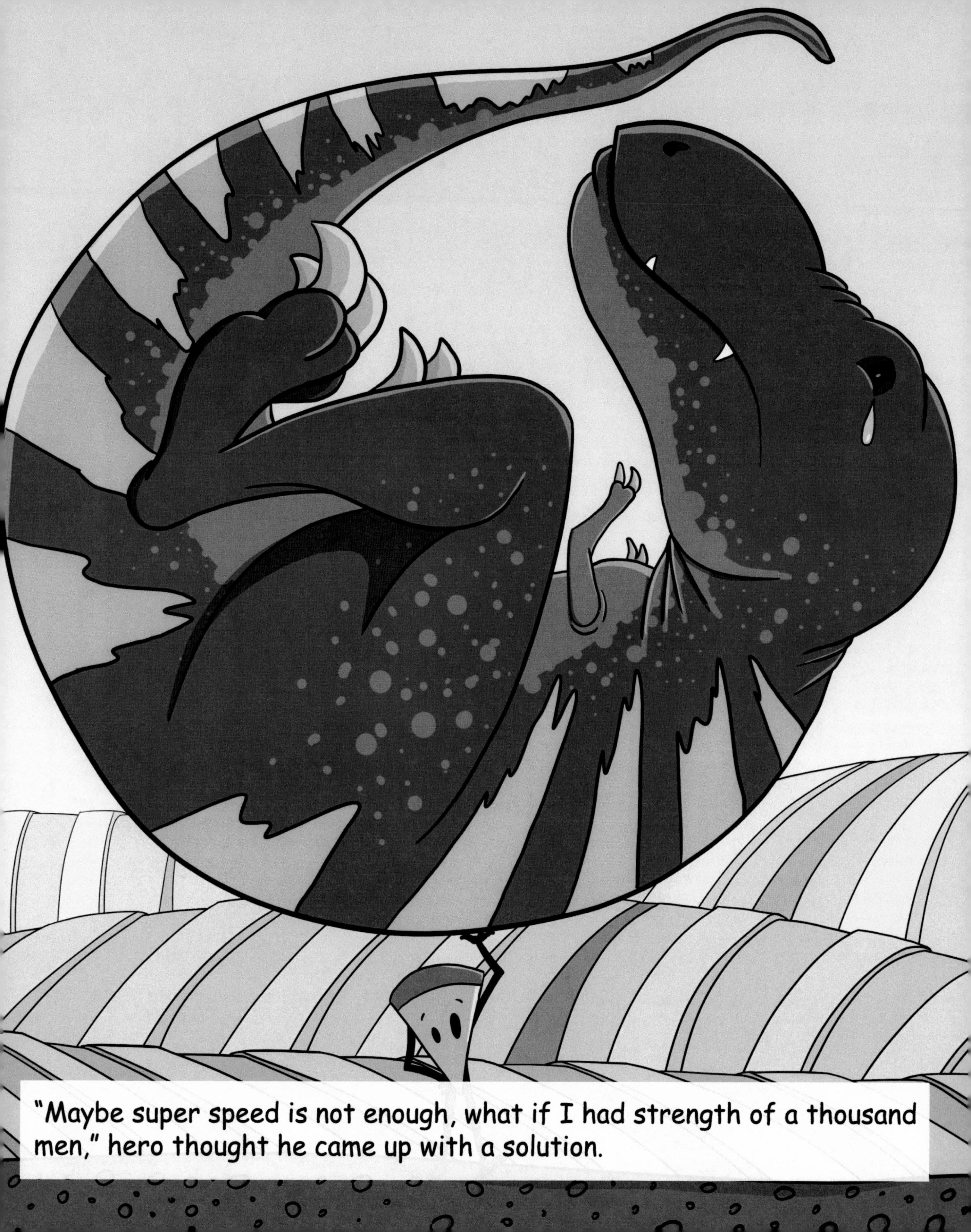

"Maybe super speed is not enough, what if I had strength of a thousand men," hero thought he came up with a solution.

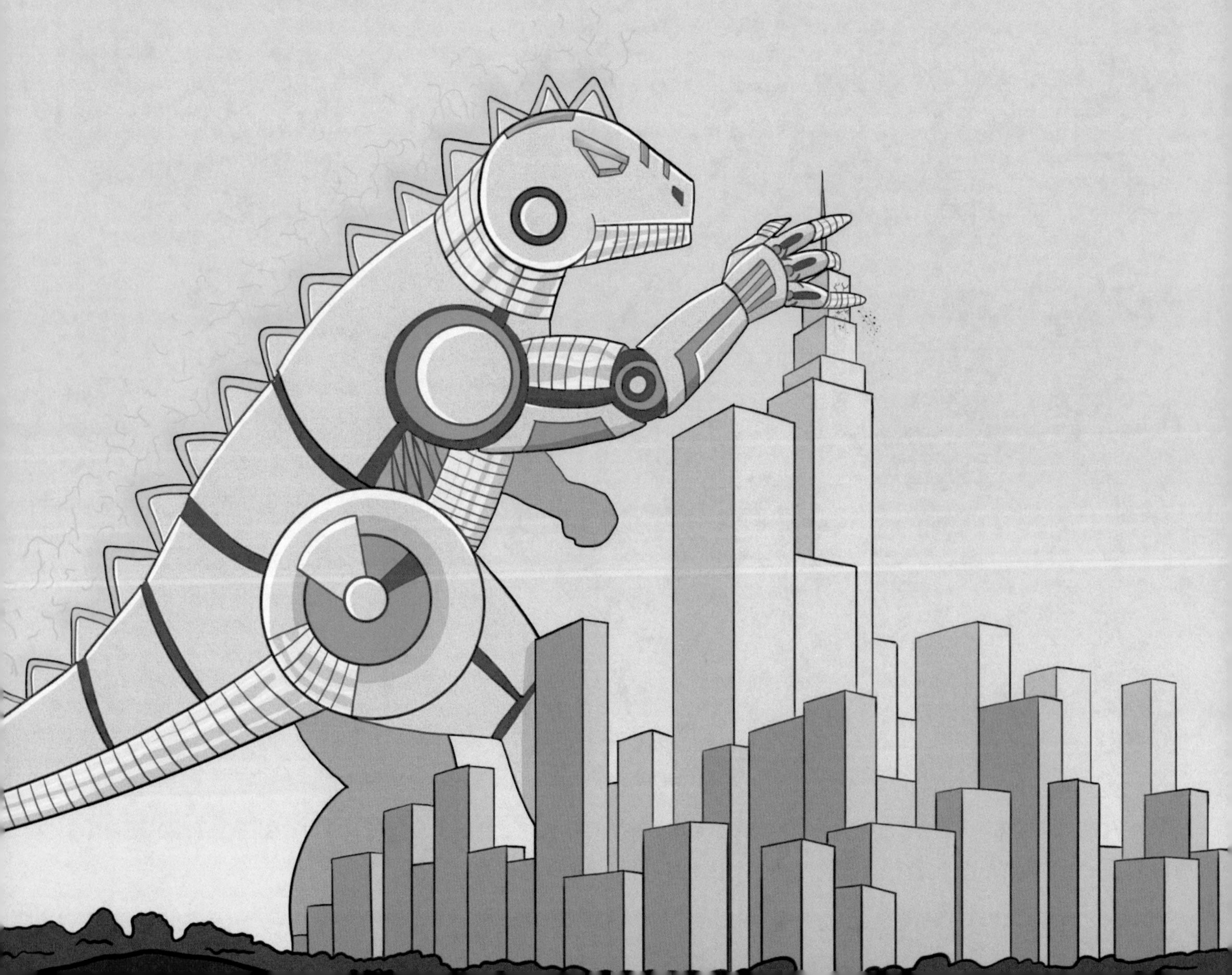

"Oh Wait! I'm back where I started. The dinosaur might as well be a lizard. I need to think quick, people are waiting for answers. What if the dinosaur was also robot? A robot so big that he stood taller than the tallest of buildings."

"Laser eyes and power of flight should even things out. The battle was glorious and lasted for hours, when finally I turned villainous robot to ash."

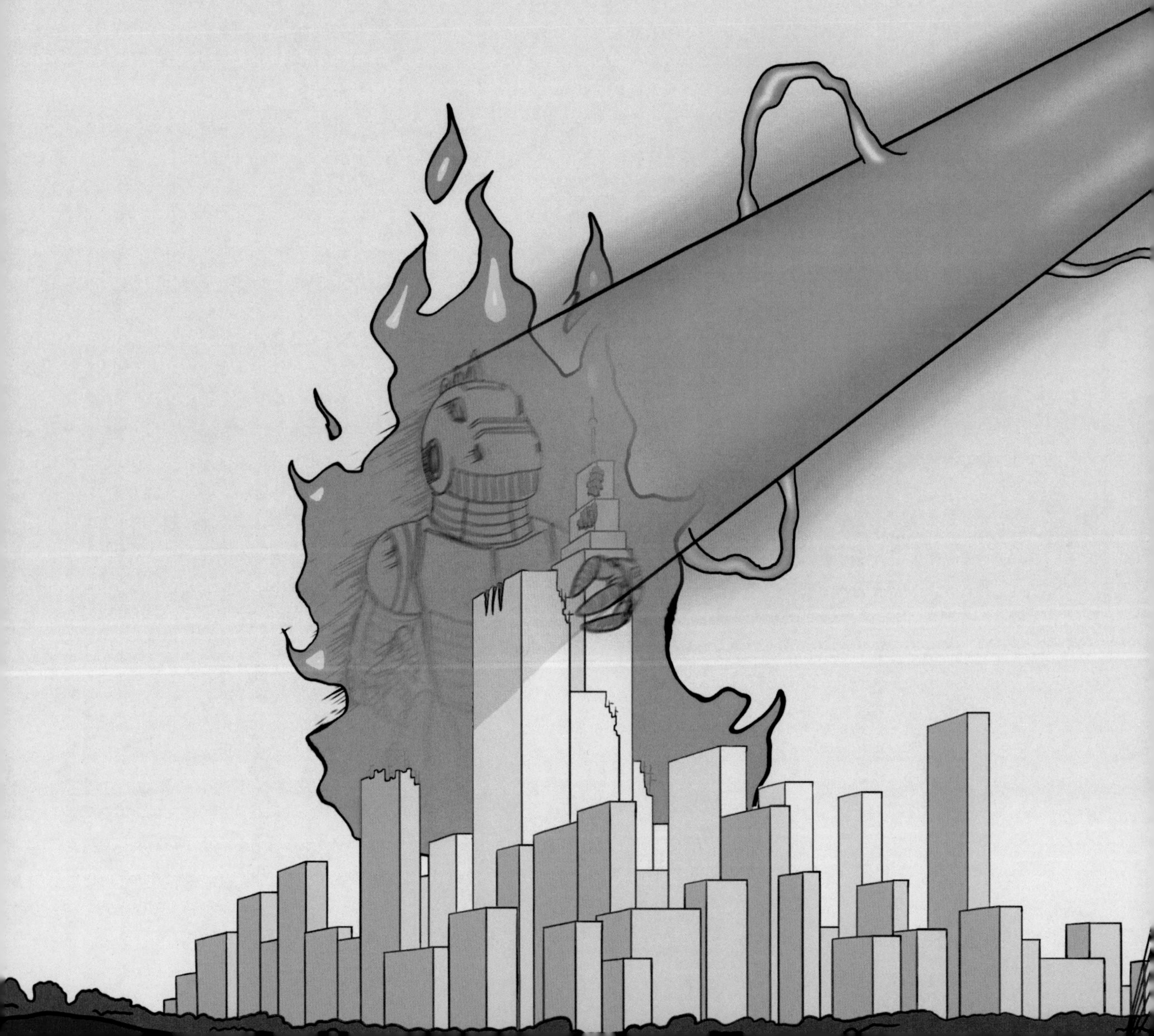

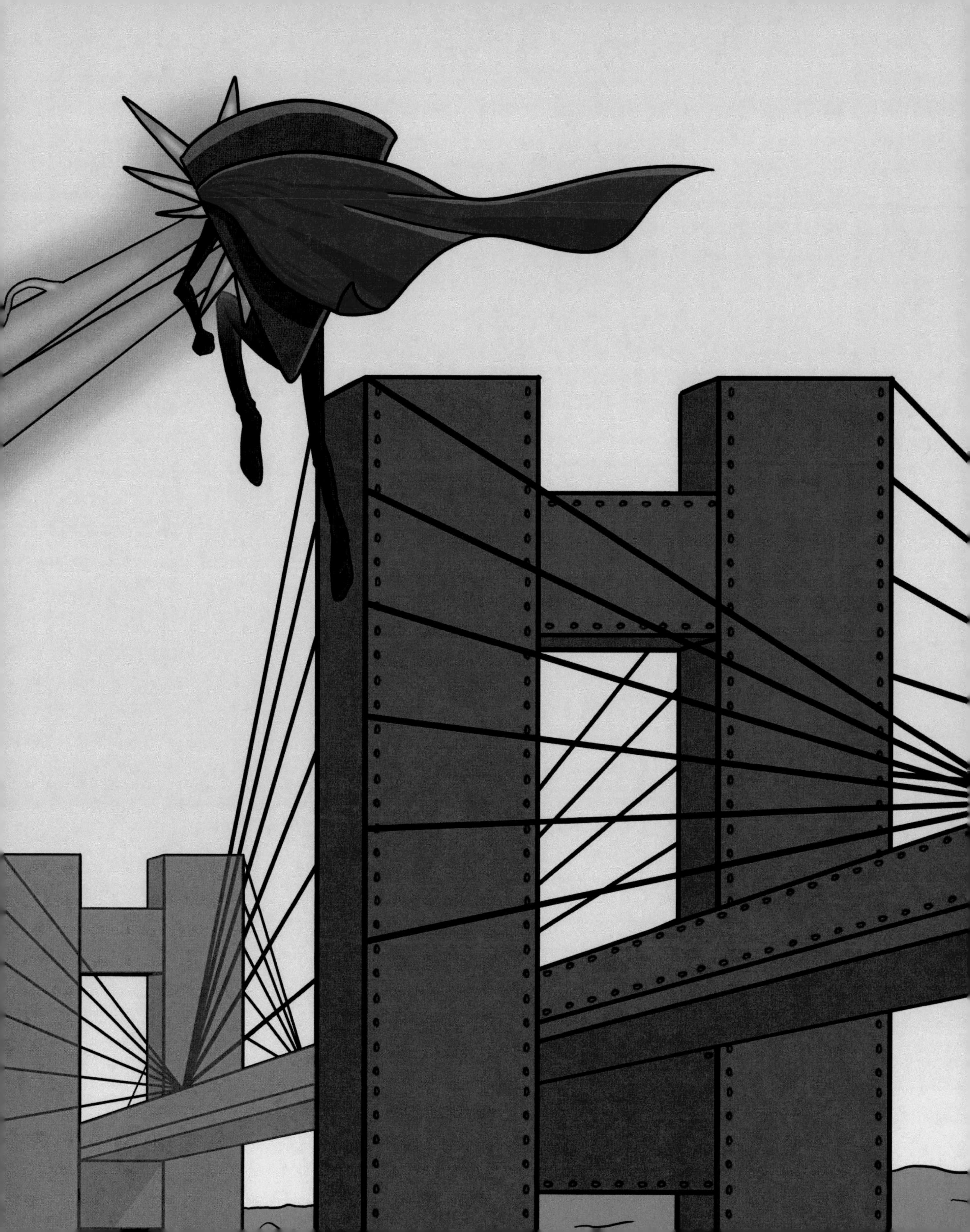

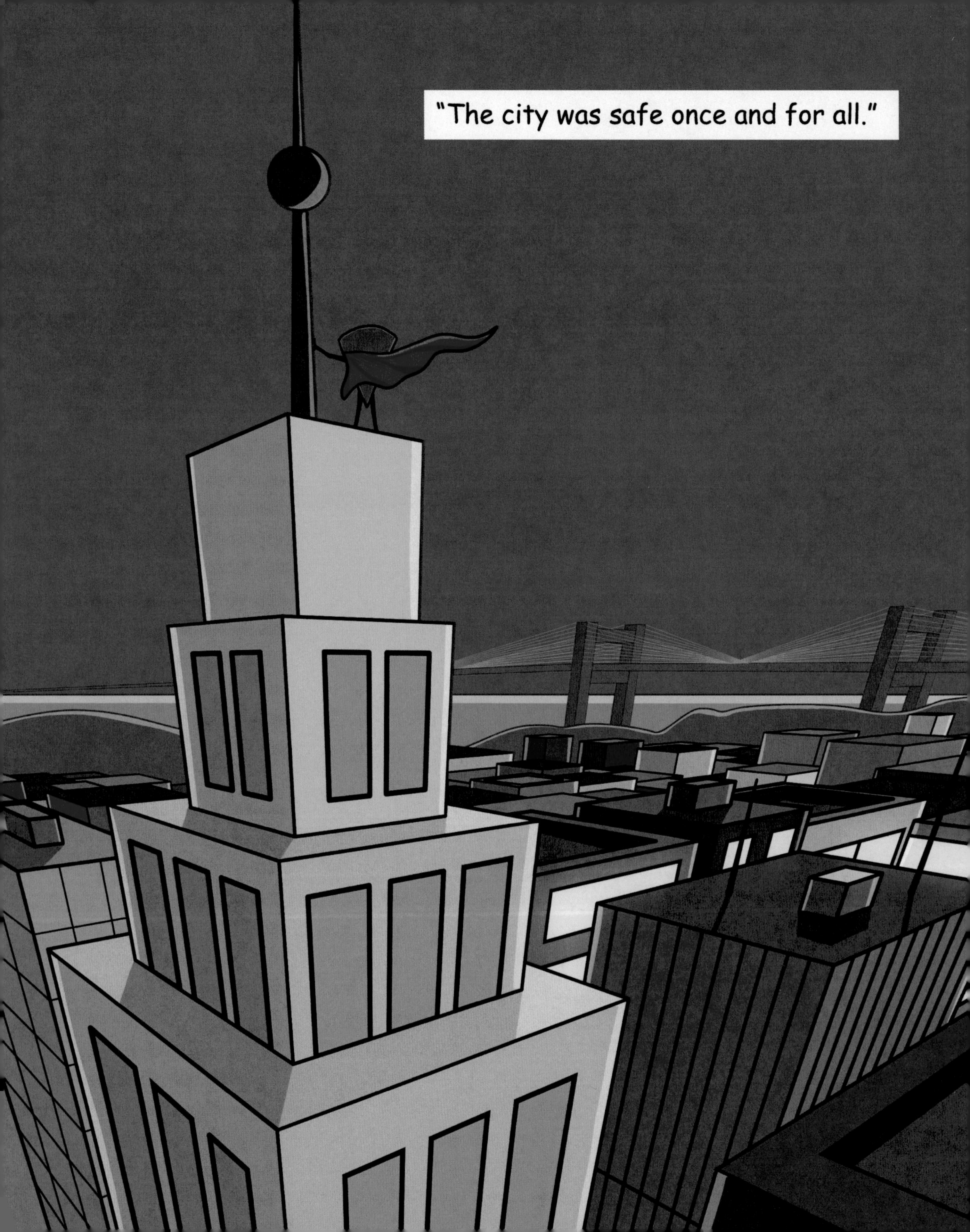
"The city was safe once and for all."

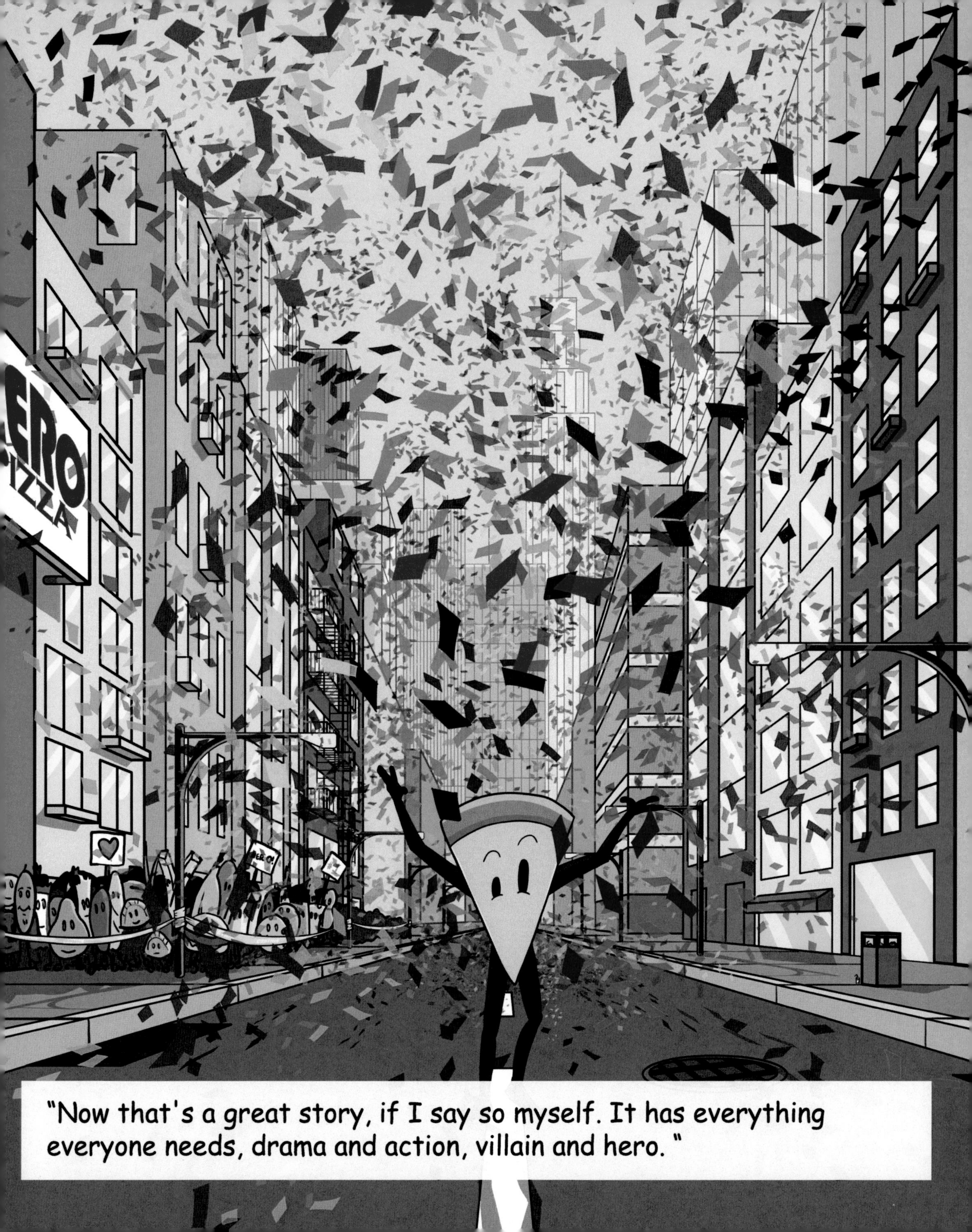
"Now that's a great story, if I say so myself. It has everything everyone needs, drama and action, villain and hero."

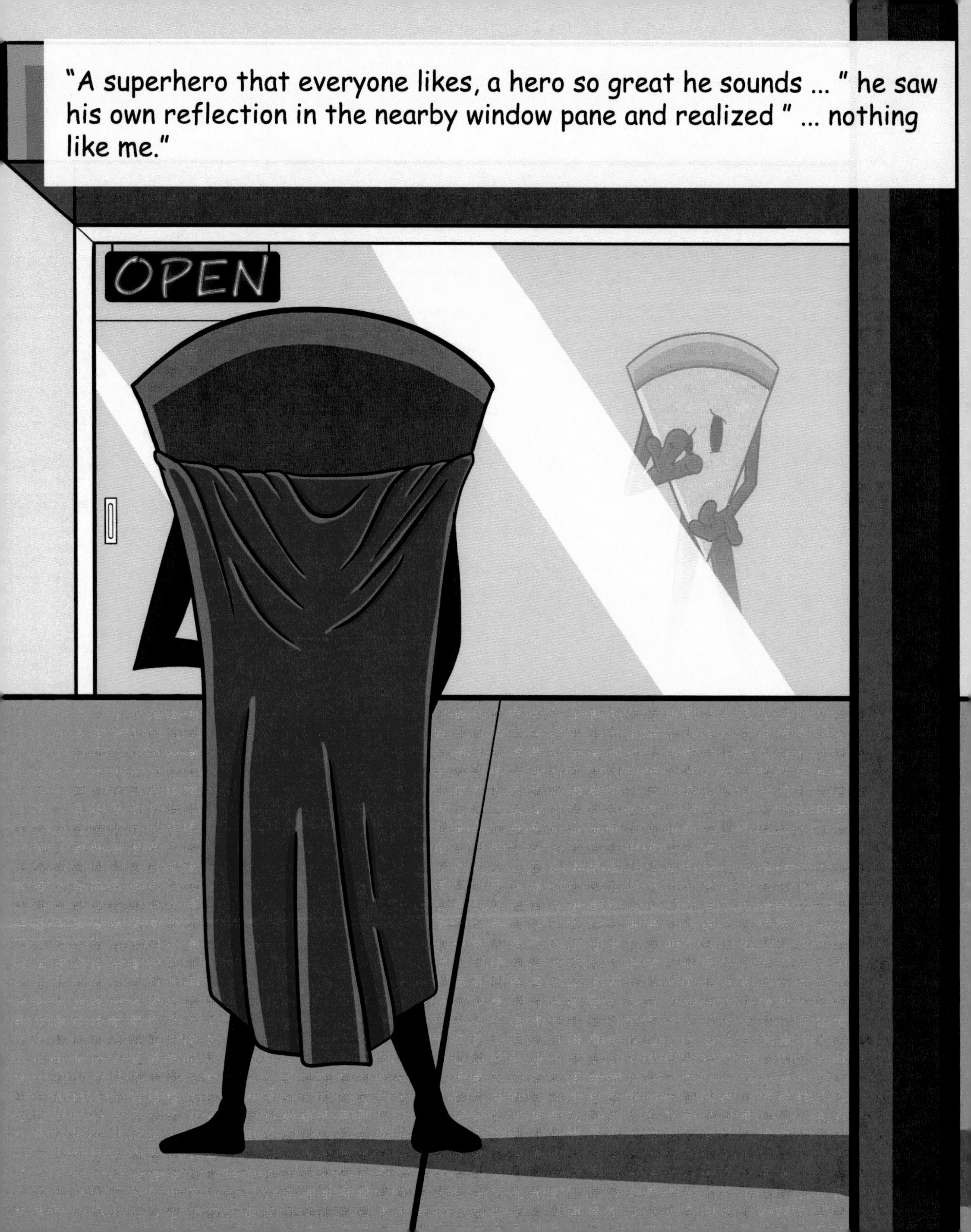
"A superhero that everyone likes, a hero so great he sounds ... " he saw his own reflection in the nearby window pane and realized " ... nothing like me."
OPEN

"What's wrong with being me?"

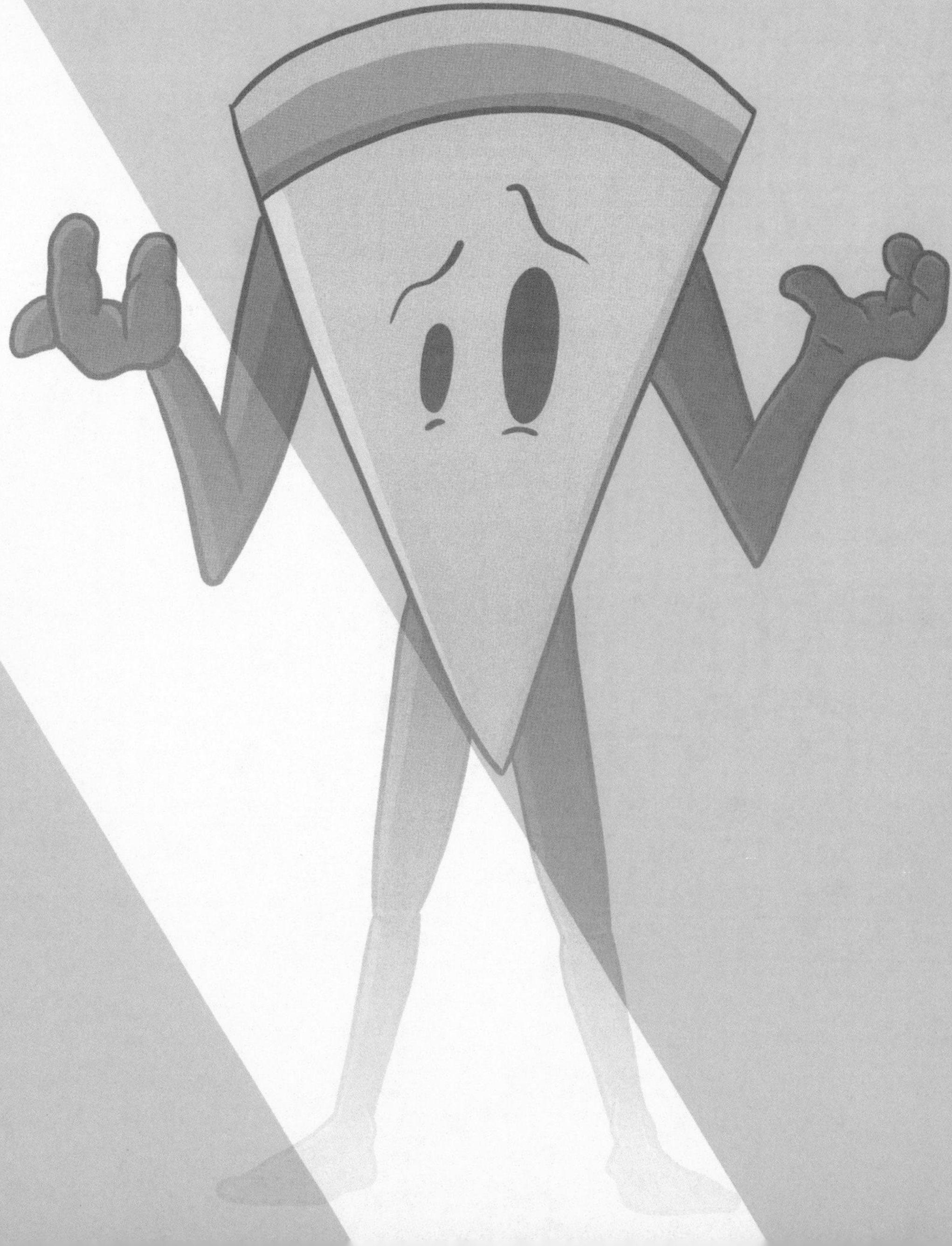

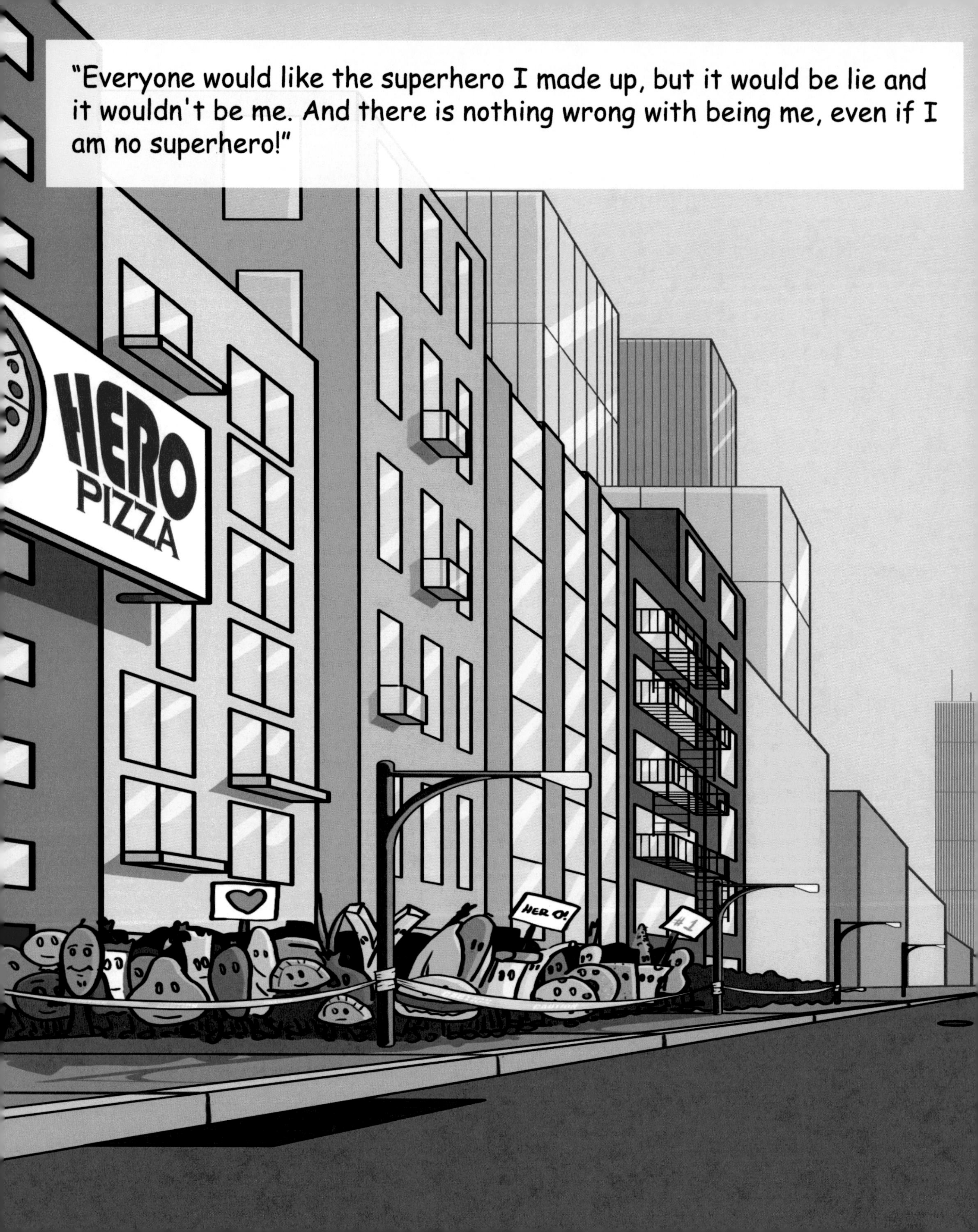
"Everyone would like the superhero I made up, but it would be lie and it wouldn't be me. And there is nothing wrong with being me, even if I am no superhero!"
HERO PIZZA
HER O!
#1

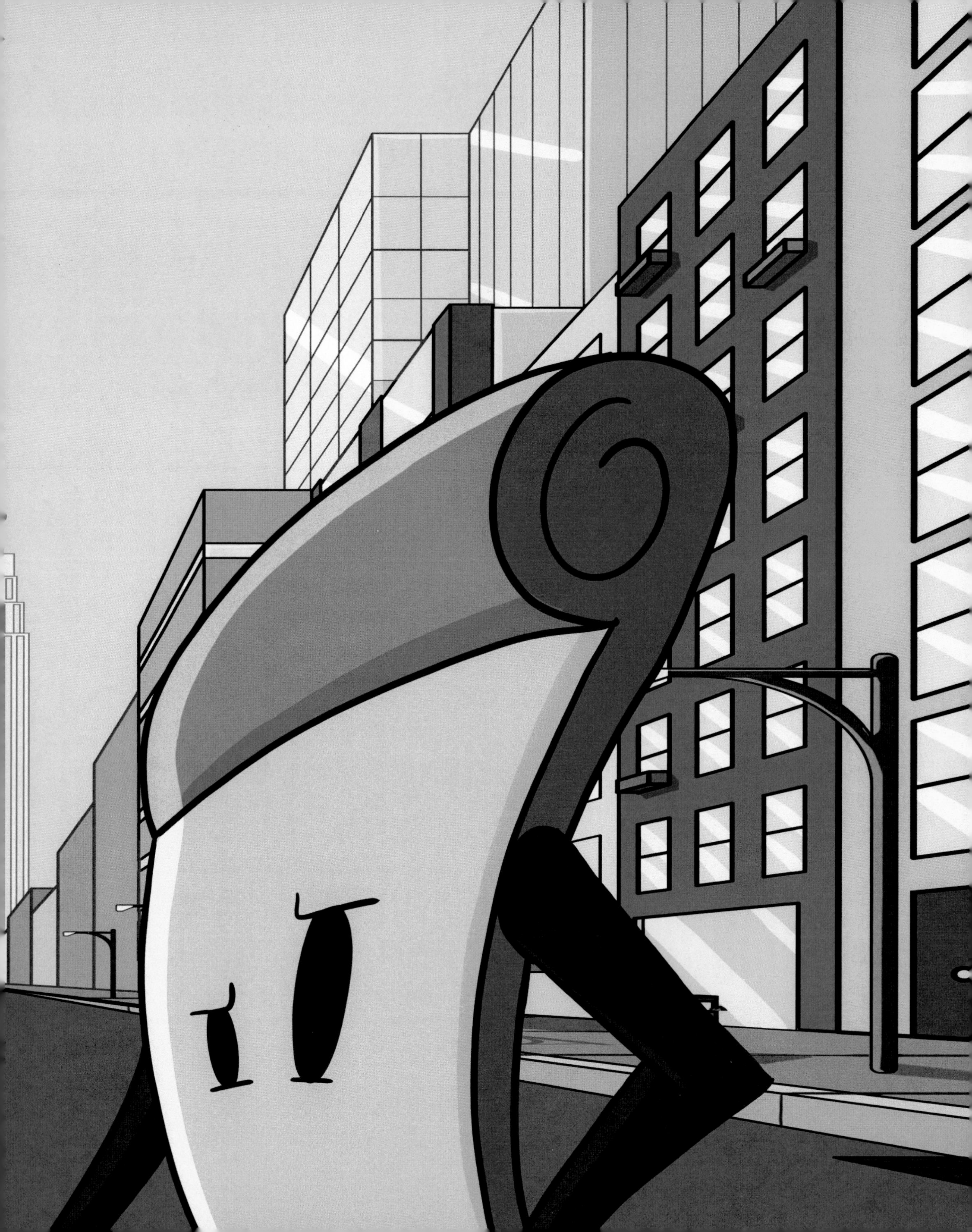

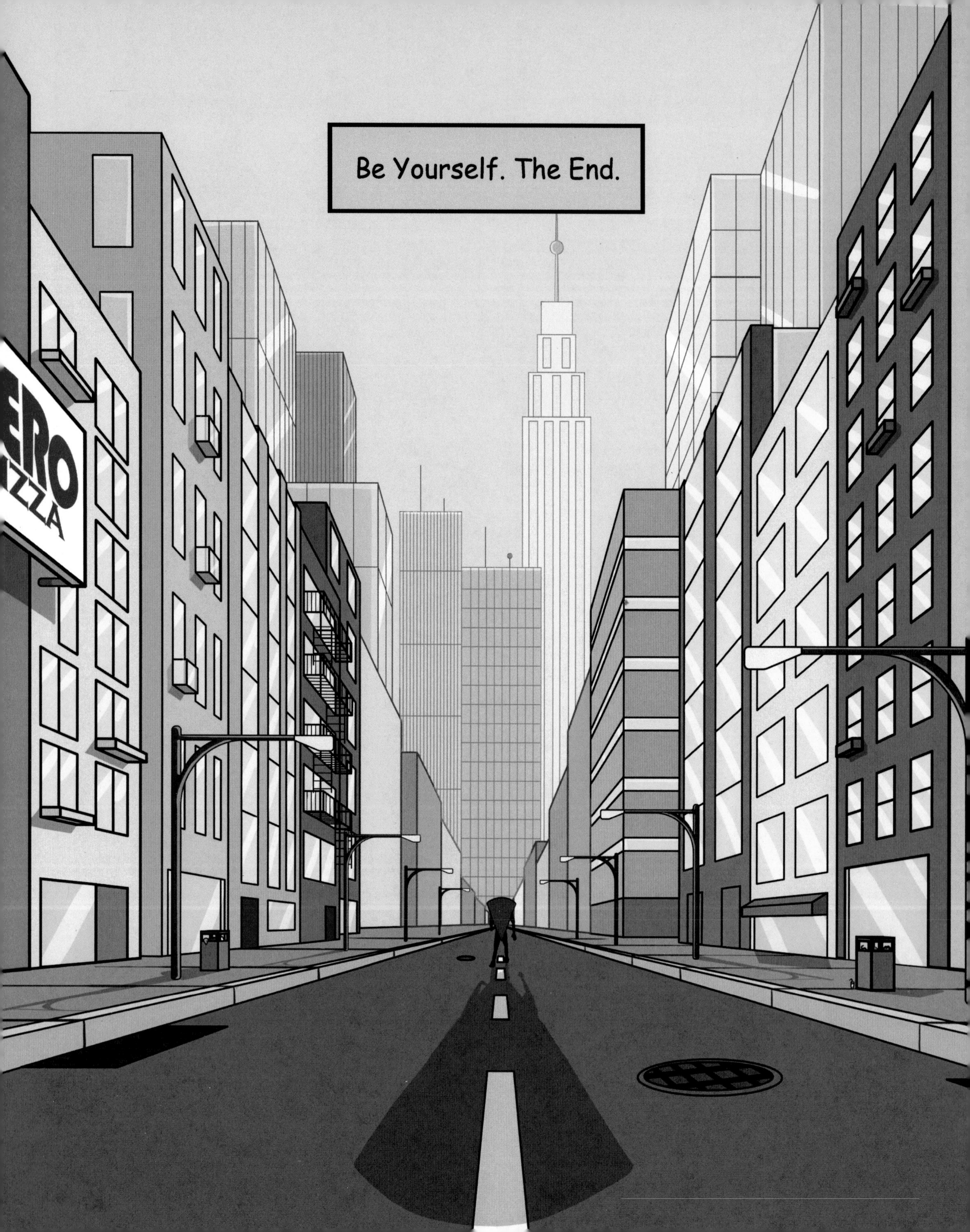
Be Yourself. The End.
ERO
IZZA